## "Oh, no," Julian whispered.
### *No, no, no*. It couldn't be!

He was close enough to the car that had pulled up to see those deep green eyes, those bouncing red curls he'd hoped never to see again.

He wanted to step back, leave. But it was too late. With a huge grin, the woman shoved open the car door.

And hit Julian square below the belt. "Ooof!" He felt waves of pain as he sank to the ground.

The woman jumped out of the car and cried, "Oh, dear!"

Julian nearly got his arms up in time as she tripped and landed right on top of him. He saw stars as their heads collided.

Blinking, fuzzy with pain, he looked up at her. "Freckles. What brings you to Hill Creek?"

"Surprise, Hawk. I'm your new medical partner."

Somehow he'd just known she was going to say that.

*C*

**Books by Cheryl Wolverton**

Love Inspired

*A Matter of Trust* #11
*A Father's Love* #20
*This Side of Paradise* #38
*The Best Christmas Ever* #47
*A Mother's Love* #63
*\*For Love of Zach* #76
*\*For Love of Hawk* #87

*Hill Creek, Texas

## CHERYL WOLVERTON

grew up in a military town though her father was no longer in the service when she was born. She attended TJHS and LHS and was attending Cameron when she met her husband, Steve. After a whirlwind courtship of two weeks they became engaged. Four months later they were married, and that was over seventeen years ago.

Cheryl and Steve have two wonderful children, Christina, sixteen, and Jeremiah, thirteen. Cheryl loves having two wonderful teenagers in the house.

As for books, Cheryl has written seven novels for the Steeple Hill Love Inspired line and is currently working on new novels. Watch for her third book in the series HILL CREEK, TEXAS, as well as other surprises planned in the future. You can contact Cheryl at P.O. Box 207, Slaughter, LA 70777. She loves to hear from readers.

# For Love
# of Hawk
## Cheryl Wolverton

*Love Inspired*®

Published by Steeple Hill Books™

STEEPLE HILL BOOKS

Steeple
Hill™

ISBN 0-373-87087-6

FOR LOVE OF HAWK

Visit us at www.steeplehill.com

**Printed in U.S.A.**

Trust in the Lord with all your heart
and lean not unto your own understanding.

—*Proverbs* 3:5

## Acknowledgments

To my doctors, Dr. John Hilton and Dr. Mary Laville.
If it wasn't for them, I'm not sure that this book
would have gotten done on time.
Thanks, guys, for being the best!

To Steeple Hill's Love Inspired e-mail group.
Goodness, their prayers over the past months have
made all the difference to me. Thank you, dear
women, for caring and having such gentle, loving
hearts. You mean the world to me.

To my friends on #theriver, an undernet IRC, yes,
even you agent and Bro Dude aka Thorn…hmmm,
one day we're going to have to learn each other's
"real" names!

And to my family who, when I was working to
finish this book up, gladly went on vacation to
Vicksburg and had a blast! Steve, keeper of my
heart, Christina and Jeremiah, my two precious
children, I love you so much.

# Chapter One

"This is where you're going to set up practice?"

Julian McCade winced when his brother Zach, the head of their family, kicked at a beat-up wastepaper basket on the cracked tiled floor. Julian had to admit it looked bad. The ancient clinic had definitely fallen into disrepair, looking more like a broken-down house of fifty years rather than a clinic that had been empty only five. "The dingy walls need a good painting, and the stale white cabinets and countertops need a good reworking—"

"Not to mention the floor," Mitch, his middle brother and sheriff of their hometown, said as he toed a loose tile with his booted foot.

Julian glanced from one brother to the other. Their look, from the top of their hair, which was as dark as his own, to the square stubborn jaws, told Julian neither brother was happy at this new development. The only difference between his two brothers was that whereas his oldest brother's blue eyes snapped with impatience, Mitch's brown ones concealed his emotions.

"This is better than using the former doctor's office. You know a lot of people from the outlying ranches and the poor had trouble getting into town where he lived. We have to go where the people are. That's why the hospital is begging for someone to reopen this clinic."

Julian felt five years old again, feeling a need to defend his actions, with both of his big brothers getting on to him. When was he going to be separate from them, a man in his own right?

Zach, at thirty-seven, stood tall and steady. His gaze traveled around the room as he took in the disaster area before him. Dark walls gritty from years of disuse faced them in the kitchen of the old Fullerton Clinic. Wallpaper that had once graced the walls now hung in loose strips.

The long wing off the kitchen, which was the actual clinic, was in a bit better shape. Still, Julian didn't like admitting Zach had a point. The kitchen was a mess. Evidently, drifters had made free use of it. If he could clean up this and the waiting room he'd have a place for patients to wait and for him to cook. The house had three small rooms set up as living quarters for who-ever ran the clinic.

Zach snorted and shifted. His hands slipped into his jeans pockets, his hat tipped lazily back on his head. Zach was firm, and it was next to impossible to get a point through to him. That was one reason Julian now turned to Mitch, hop-ing for help. He should have known better.

Mitch, in his tan sheriff's uniform, hat in hand, looked downright belligerent.

"We just busted a drug gang, Julian. You don't need to be out here alone—"

"The hospital is hiring a partner," Julian pointed out patiently, having learned not to get ornery with his brothers—especially when they were both on the same side.

"I think it's wonderful that you'll be out here for them."

*Laura.* The last occupant of the room. Julian glanced over at the willowy blond woman and smiled. Of everyone here, she had been on his side backing him up since he had returned to the area two weeks ago. After nearly losing her brother out here, his sister-in-law understood the necessity to move farther out into the wilderness.

She also had backed Julian when both brothers had wanted him living out at the old homestead instead of here. Laura had informed them that as an adult on his own for several semesters now, he might have other ideas about just where he wanted to live. When she had backed him after his brothers had immediately nixed the idea of his opening the run-down clinic, he had decided he really liked his sister-in-law.

She had actually challenged Zach and gotten him to agree to come out and at least look at the place.

And now, the way Zach was looking at his wife, Julian realized Laura just might succeed in getting his oldest brother off his back. Things here in Hill Creek had certainly changed since he'd been away at medical school.

"Well, my deputy might be able to talk you into agreeing, Zach." Mitch's voice intruded into Julian's thoughts. "But she isn't going to be changing my mind." Mitch turned his dark eyes from Zach to Julian and frowned severely. "Jul, the place out here is dangerous. This is the very property the DEA caught the drug smugglers on, the same ones who almost murdered your sister-in-law.''

''As I heard it,'' Julian said coolly, ''it was your old deputy who did that.''

Mitch bristled.

Laura interrupted. ''You're right. It was Harry who shot me, but he did work for the smugglers, too. However, Julian, that's not the point. The point is, your brothers are simply worried about you. How about a compromise?''

Both Zach and Mitch looked warily at Laura. Julian didn't care that they stared at her as if she'd suddenly called fire down on them. He grabbed the chance to get both brothers off his back. ''What type of compromise?'' he encouraged Laura.

''You let your brothers and friends fix up the kitchen and private quarters, let them have the phone turned on, the tanks filled and everything that will make basic survival out here safe. Then they'll back off and allow you to do what you want.''

Julian glared. She was on his side? He didn't think so. That plan might make sense to someone else. But not to him.

He didn't want to depend on his brothers at all. He had no desire to let them interfere in anything he did. He wanted to prove to them he could do it all. He wasn't going to let them meddle.

Of course, he wasn't a bit surprised when *they* agreed to the idea.

"Sounds good to me," Zach said, smiling at his wife. When had Zach gone so soft? Julian wondered.

"I still don't like it," Mitch muttered.

Zach gave Mitch the superior I'm-the-oldest look.

"But I'll go along with it," Mitch added reluctantly.

"Well, I hate to disappoint you, but I won't," Julian said, interrupting their mutual agreements.

"What?" all three said in unison, turning to stare at him. Laura looked shocked. Zach stared with an inscrutable look. And Mitch, well, Mitch scowled as if he was angry again.

Taking a deep breath, Julian forged ahead with what he hadn't told them before, the news that would really upset them. "I've already talked to the hospital, and I've talked with the bank. Dr. Gonzales thinks the site is ideal, and the bank has loaned me enough money to get started."

Zach    frowned,    his    features    darkening.

"You've already decided? Before you even got us out here?"

"It was my decision," Julian said firmly. Man, he thought, facing down a gang intent on getting to one of his patients was easier than facing his two brothers.

"It's not just *your* decision but *our* decision," Zach said in a low voice. "What you do affects this family. We should have at least been consulted."

"I'm fully grown. I don't have to consult you on what I do."

Laura glanced between the brothers. "Let's all just calm down."

Zach paused, then nodded. "Fine. I'll be at the ranch if he comes to his senses." Turning, he strode out the door.

"You'll be at the ranch a long time, then," Julian called after his brother.

Mitch shook his head and stalked off after his older brother.

Laura sighed and gave Julian one of those looks totally reserved for a five-year-old who has done something bad and knows it. At least she didn't shake her finger at him, but the way she shook her head made him wonder if that meant the same thing. "Be good, Julian. Now I have to go handle a bear. He only loves you."

"Well, he doesn't have to smother me," he told Laura, again feeling frustrated and angry with his older brothers and not sure why.

Laura's frown faded and she moved forward, laying a gentle hand on Julian's arm. Her eyes asked him to understand, to listen. "You're lucky you have someone who cares."

Julian lifted his other hand and placed it over her smaller one, his dark skin making hers look that much lighter. He liked his sister-in-law. She was gentle, tender, caring. He didn't know anyone like that. She really cared about Zach, Mitch and even him. Her next words confirmed just how much her new family meant to her. "Don't let it end like this. The Bible tells us not to let the sun set on our wrath."

Julian gave in. Who wouldn't when someone like Laura gave him such an entreating look? With a reluctant nod, he acquiesced. "Very well."

Laura's face glowed like a brightly lit Christmas tree on a cold dark night.

No wonder Zach couldn't resist Laura. Julian was certainly glad this woman wasn't his problem. He had a feeling he'd give her whatever she asked, too. "Okay, okay. Turn off the joy, Laura. I'm doing it."

She hugged him, chuckling, and then stepped back. "You catch on faster than Mitch, but don't tell him I said that." She winked.

Julian simply shook his head before sprinting out the door. He easily spotted Zach. In the overgrown dirt parking lot, there were only two vehicles besides his—Zach's dusty forest-green truck and Mitch's 4×4, which was black and brown and sitting next to his sporty red hatchback. "Hey, Zach, wait."

Zach paused at the truck, his gaze cutting back to Julian. "Yeah?"

"Look," Julian began. He didn't want to give in, but he also didn't want strife between them. Since Zach had raised them after their parents had been killed in a freak skydiving accident, Zach had been more than just a brother. Zach was the foundation of a world turned topsy-turvy. When they could have been broken up and sent to different homes, at nineteen Zach fought to keep the family together, to keep them all in church and to keep them all at home.

"Don't leave angry," Julian said. And meant it this time.

Zach had succeeded in keeping them together,

and Julian admired and loved his brother for that. But Julian had no desire to stay here—especially if it meant staying and facing a family rift that he had caused.

"I have a debt to pay to the county hospital. I signed that agreement when they let me work my last year of high school training with their doctors in that special jump-start program. You know that. And you know I'll be here two years."

He'd promised the hospital five years of service, or two years in a branch clinic that he would run if his grades were high. He'd graduated fifteenth in his class of five hundred. So he had two years of service he owed Hill Creek County Memorial Hospital before his debt was considered paid and he could move on to greener pastures.

"I simply want to fulfill my contract. And a clinic is the best way to do that. You know we need it." Two years would also be long enough to show his brothers he didn't need their help every time he made a decision. Then he'd be off to chase his dream.

"Two years before you leave," Zach muttered.

"Two years he'll be with us," Laura cor-

rected from behind Julian before she walked
over and slipped an arm through Zach's. She
smiled sweetly up at him.

"Will you stop that?" Mitch drawled, the
heat gone from his voice and the good humor
restored. "You know he can't think when you
look at him like that."

"Yeah, I do." Laura grinned smugly and
squeezed Zach's arm.

Zach's frown eased into a soft smile and he
chuckled. "Not true," he murmured.

"But it *is* true that your brother is back. He'll
be here for two years. And fighting isn't the way
God wants you to start out Julian's return."

Zach leaned down and kissed Laura on the tip
of her nose. "You're right, sweetheart." Shifting his weight, he pivoted toward Julian. "I
apologize, Julian, for my attitude. We want you
back and..." As if realizing going any further
would only start the argument back, he hesitated.

"And—" Laura jumped in "—we'll be glad
to support you in this project. Right?"

Zach tipped his hat back and looked up at the
sky. "Women."

"You married her." Mitch's voice rang with
amusement.

"You hired her," Zach retorted. "Okay,

okay. Of course we'll support you. You know that. We'd just like to know what's going on with you, not find out after the fact. How would you feel if the hospital hired a partner for you and didn't tell you until that partner arrived? You'd be frustrated, upset, angry, wouldn't you?''

Slowly Julian shook his head. "Not at all. Why do you think that? A partner is a partner. Why would I care, as long as the doctor was a good doctor? And to work out here, the hospital wants only the top graduates. So, I have nothing to worry about.''

"Give it up, big bro.'' Mitch shook his head and started toward his 4×4. "He's not going to give in.''

"Well, that's how we felt,'' Zach continued, ignoring Mitch's advice. Julian watched the way he slipped his arm around Laura, so casually, absently, pulling her up against his side and squeezing her. He silently thanked God that Zach had finally found someone.

"Hey, someone's coming this way,'' Mitch interrupted, pointing toward a dust cloud in the distance on the driveway that led out to the ranch—a driveway that was nearly forty-five minutes long.

Julian lifted a hand, shielding his eyes against the midday glare of the winter sun. Sure enough, someone certainly was headed toward them. As the car got closer he saw it was a beat-up old Volkswagen bug, gunmetal gray, the paint having worn off a long time before, similar to his old truck he had in the barn here at this clinic. But this car...

Why did that car seem vaguely familiar and cause a feeling of dread to work its way up his spine? Julian wondered.

"Wonder who it is," Zach murmured as the car came closer.

"Not from around here. I'd know the car," Mitch replied.

"Oh, no," Julian suddenly whispered. *No, no, no.* It couldn't be. He took two steps toward the vehicle that turned into the parking lot. The dust swirled up around the car, but not enough to block the bright red curls that bounced as the woman twisted the wheel and came to an abrupt stop next to him.

He was close enough to see her eyes, those deep green eyes he'd thought—hoped—he'd never see again. Then she grinned, that bright, infectious grin that lured every person in, encouraged them to be at ease, until she went in for the kill.

"She seems to know you," Laura said as she started forward.

He wanted to warn Laura to stay back, to leave and find somewhere else to go, but it was too late. With a huge grin, the woman waved again and shoved open the door.

And hit Julian right square below the belt. "Oooaf."

He heard his own groan, felt the waves of pain as he grabbed himself and sank to the ground. Both brothers shouted and started forward, but he ignored them. Through the haze of pain he saw the familiar wince as the woman jumped out of the car, and then heard her cry, "Oh, dear! I didn't mean that."

Julian sank the rest of the way to the ground and smiled through a tight face. "Of course you didn't, Freckles."

"You know her?" Zach asked, and it was nice to hear the note of wariness in his voice, see the look of pity in his eyes.

Before he could answer, though, the woman came forward. "Oh, yes. We know each other well. I'm a doctor. Let me through. I'll see if he's oka-a-a-ay—"

Julian managed to get his arms up just in time to catch the woman as she tripped and landed on top of him.

He saw stars as their heads collided.

She gasped and then grabbed his shoulders.

He really didn't want to focus on her. He simply wanted to believe it was a dream, no, a nightmare. Yes, a nightmare was much better than reality right now.

She grunted as her slightly plump body shifted.

Blinking, he looked up at her. "Freckles."

Her eyes were still a bit fuzzy with pain, but at her nickname, Susan finally focused on him.

"What brings you here?" he asked, his head throbbing to the tune of freck-les, freck-les, freck-les, the tune it had throbbed to many times before.

Susan reached up and rubbed her forehead before answering. "Surprise, Hawk. I'm your new partner."

Somehow, he'd known she was going to say that.

# Chapter Two

"Hawk?"

Horribly embarrassed, Susan Learner pushed herself awkwardly off Julian McCade. She had been so nervous about seeing him again. Oh, why had she tripped and fallen on him?

She accepted the large tan hand of the sheriff. Stumbling to her feet, she balanced herself by putting a hand to the sheriff's chest.

Her eyes widened.

He wore the same last name as Hawk. It couldn't be...she looked from the tag to his dark eyes, to the tag, to his high cheekbones and curved lips, to the name tag....

Smiling sickly, she whispered, "Nice name

tag." Releasing him, she stepped back and brushed herself off, deciding her best defense was to pretend none of it had happened. After all, Hawk was still in one piece. As was she. That was the most important thing. With a bright smile, she turned to the one who had asked the question, the only other man present—and realized he was a very big, formidable man. "Hawk. Everyone calls him Hawk. Hawk McCade, that is."

She wasn't sure why the man was staring at her as if she'd spoken Spanish or some obscure foreign language. And his eyes... She looked from Julian to Mitch and then at Zach, then back at Mitch. No, she wasn't going to ask. Looking down at Julian, she smiled. "Isn't that right?" This couldn't be another brother. There couldn't be three of them so drop-dead gorgeous in the same family, except that the cheekbones, and the eyes, and the dark skin... No, no way. That couldn't be his other brother.

Julian staggered to his feet. She thought about helping him brush himself off, but remembered the last time she'd done that. It had taken the teacher thirty minutes to get the fire out, and the entire building had been evacuated. Of course, she wasn't the one who had jumped and knocked over the flammable liquid next to the Bunsen burner, she thought, silently defending herself.

Those dark eyes of his—they just did something to her every time she looked into them. With a dreamy sigh, she realized she still wasn't over her feelings for Hawk McCade.

Then she heard the two men laughing. And Hawk had that wary look plastered firmly in place as he stared at her. "Why are they laughing, Hawk?"

"I knew you hated your name, Julian...but Hawk?" Sheriff McCade hooted and slapped his hat against his leg. "What do you think about that, Zach? Hawk!"

Zach tried to smother a laugh, but Susan saw it.

"You stop laughing at him," Susan said, and started forward, shaking a finger at the sheriff. "You should be ashamed. An officer of the law, giving the doctor a bad time, the very man who one day may hold your life in his hands. Or me—I'm a doctor, too, and don't like one of my colleagues being laughed at."

"Whoa..." Mitch threw up his hands and backpedaled from her.

She was glad, until she felt the firm grip on

her arm. She knew that grip so well. "It's okay, Freckles. That's my brother Mitch."

Turning, she saw Julian's long-suffering look and realized she'd done something wrong again. "He shouldn't have made fun of your name. That name is an honor."

Julian frowned. "Well, yeah. But you know how older brothers are."

Susan smiled and shook her head. "I'm the oldest of six, remember?"

"I don't think I knew that."

Susan didn't tell him that was the first personal question he'd asked her. No, she didn't want to push her luck. After all their time in medical school, he had finally spoken to her. Maybe she wasn't crazy to have accepted this job knowing he was the one she'd be working with, the very man she had fallen for upon first sight.

"So, are you going to introduce us?"

Julian smiled at the woman and nodded. "This is my brother Zach and his wife, Laura. Laura, Zach, this is Susan Learner, someone who graduated from our medical school. Mitch, I think you've already met her," he said, a tiny smirk on his face.

Zach came forward, hand extended. "Nice to meet you, Dr. Learner."

Susan smiled at the title. Doctor. That sounded so nice. A beautiful title that she had rarely heard until now. "Please call me Susan," she said, and shook his hand. And that it was one of Hawk's brothers...one of the men who had just seen what a klutz she was...

"You're assigned here?" Laura asked. She came forward and shook Susan's hand.

"Yes. I needed somewhere to work off my loan for school. This place was one of the areas that had requested a doctor. So, I'm here for an indeterminate amount of time."

Mitch stepped forward and shook her hand. "We can always use an extra doctor out here."

"Thank you," she said, accepting his hand. "My mouth does tend to run off without me. I hope you'll forgive my abrupt words."

Mitch grinned, two large dimples, so much like Julian's, appearing. There was no doubt they were related. "No problem at all, Dr. Learner—Susan," he corrected himself. "It's good to know someone is watching out for our little brother."

Julian scowled.

Susan sighed. That was definitely the wrong

thing to say to Julian. She gathered from his look that the idea of her watching out for him was something he didn't like at all.

"Well," Susan said, breaking into the tense silence, "do I get a tour of the clinic? Or do I explore it myself?"

Julian nodded. "That's your cue to leave, guys. I should show my associate around."

"You'll be over later for dinner," Zach said matter-of-factly.

"Yes," Julian said, exasperation rife in his words. "I'll be there. At least until I can get this kitchen fixed up."

"Susan, you're invited, too," Laura said as she headed toward the truck.

"Oh, I—I'm not sure—" she began, only to be interrupted by Mitch.

"It's the code of the West. You're invited. Have Julian bring you. As soon as you're all set up, we'll ease off."

She simply shook her head. Having come from New York City, this cordiality was just too unusual for her. Finally, with a nod, she accepted. "Thank you."

Laura winked at Julian. "Now, if you were only so gracious. We'll see you then."

Susan heard Julian mumble something and

watched the three people wander off to their vehicles and leave. It wasn't until they started down the road that Susan turned to Julian and smiled.

"You knew about this assignment before you left, didn't you?" he asked mildly.

"Now, Hawk," Susan said.

Julian simply stared at the redhead, watching the way her freckles suddenly stood out at her words. He couldn't believe Freckles Learner was standing in front of him. "Don't you 'now, Hawk' me, Freckles. You knew, didn't you?"

Susan shrugged. "Of course I did. But knowing you, I decided the better part of survival was not to mention it to you until I showed up."

Julian barely kept from groaning. Susan must have sensed his reaction, because she bristled up like an outraged mother hen.

"Those accidents in school are all over, Hawk. I needed a job that was stable, something challenging, something that would pay enough for me to make money to pay off my school loans and then some. This job paid surprisingly better than many."

"That, my dear, is because you have to live out in the wilderness and it's very primitive compared to what we've been taught."

"We interned at that emergency room together," Susan muttered. "That was certainly primitive."

"Ha. Just wait until you see this." Julian turned and motioned her toward the building.

"I noticed the yard is overgrown and, well, they have posts lining the side of the building."

"Those wooden posts on the side of the building are to tie up horses. Many patients out here rode horses to visit the doctor. When I was a kid, the doctor used to keep the horses there—separate from the truck parking."

She paused, looking up at the building. "Two stories," she murmured. "Nice size. The outside could use a good scrubbing, though."

"That's stucco. It's supposed to look like that," Julian said. He pulled the door open and stepped back to let her enter first. He wasn't disappointed when her jaw dropped.

When she nearly tripped over a loose tile going inside, he was there to right her.

He quickly released her and kept his distance. Getting too close to her wasn't good. Touching her was worse.

"The walls...they're yellow...." Her eyes widened as she turned in circles, taking in the entire lobby. "And no one has worked here in years!" she finally added.

Julian chuckled. "That's right, Freckles. Congratulations," he said, patting her shoulder as he moved on in and walked past her. "Because you're the person who gets to help me reopen this clinic." If he'd hoped to send her running, he failed.

Instead, her green eyes lost the shocked look and glowed with sudden purpose. "You know, if we clean this front room and then the offices—we have filing cabinets there by the desk and I have a computer. How are we going to set up on equipment?"

"Whoa." Julian held up a hand. "Look, Freckles, I wasn't expecting you. I was kidding. I just finished examining the clinic myself." Shaking his head, he decided seeing would be better than telling. "Come this way."

Guiding her down the hall to the offices and the treatment rooms, he showed her the shape each one was in.

"This is archaic." Raising her green gaze to his own brown one, she shook her head. "Obsolete."

"The hospital has agreed to supply the basics—X-ray, blood equipment. The more serious testing has to be sent to Hill Creek County. And if it's really bad, then they'll have to be airlifted out to a bigger hospital.''

''Everything is so far away.'' Susan walked over to the window, pulled back a ragged piece of cloth that had once been a curtain and looked out over the Texas landscape. Julian could imagine what an outsider would think looking out that window. Bleak, where empty space stretched for miles. Few could handle it. Even having grown up here he had trouble handling it sometimes.

''That was never a problem in New York. I can see now why the hospital agreed to reopen this clinic,'' Susan finally said, and turned around, new determination in her eyes, her posture.

''You have no idea how important this clinic is. My sister-in-law almost lost her brother out here in the wilderness. We lose people every year because they can't make it into the hospital, or just won't travel that far. Many of the poorer people don't have the means to get there. Some don't even own a car.''

Susan nodded, understanding well what poor meant. Thinking of her own family back home and the money she was sending them, she wondered if Hawk would truly understand what it felt like to go without. Eventually she would make enough money to help her family get out of the bad neighborhood they lived in.

As Susan looked around, she thought even if it meant working here in a place like this, so far away from home and everything familiar, she'd do it. Of course, the added benefit was she'd get to work with Hawk.

She whispered a silent prayer that God would guide her steps. For some reason, every time she got near Hawk, she turned into a bumbling idiot. Like earlier.

"When do we meet with the hospital about the equipment we'll need?"

Susan saw Hawk wince at the word *we*. She ignored it.

"Tomorrow. I've taken care of a lot of the basics. The small section of the second floor we have will have to wait to be fixed up. It was mainly a storage area anyway. We should be able to get the rest ready for work in two weeks, maybe three. It'll definitely be open before the holidays."

Susan nodded. "Thanksgiving and Christmas." A pang of loneliness hit her. Not wanting to think about it, she changed the subject. "So, is there a hotel in Hill Creek? Somewhere I can stay until I find an apartment?''

"Apartment?'' His face twisted into a parody of disbelief. "You've never lived out in the country like this, have you?''

"Well, no,'' she said a bit defensively. It's not as if she'd asked to move into the Ritz Carlton. Surely they had small rooms or something that they sublet.

"No apartments. There might be someone willing to rent out part of their house. Other than that, you aren't going to find anywhere to stay.''

"Oh.'' Susan frowned, not willing to show her uneasiness and fear. She suddenly felt way out of place here.

"But you don't have to worry about that. If you'll read the contract you signed, you'll be living in at the clinic. They provide us a residence and a kitchen.''

"But I can't live in here until it's habitable.'' She was appalled that the hospital hadn't told her that.

"Dr. Gonzales hasn't spoken with you, has he?'' Julian shook his head. "Everything should have been arranged with you already. My brother, the sheriff, volunteered the ranch to put up people working at the clinic, since it's so close. Wonder if Mitch has told Zach yet,'' he murmured, and two dimples cut down the sides of his dark skin, giving him a boyish look. ''Anyway, you, the workers if they're not from this area and anyone else will all be welcome at the ranch house. However, Zach will gladly put you and me up.''

''They'll just open their houses up like that?'' Susan asked, amazed. Where she came from, people just didn't do that.

''Yes, Freckles, they do. Not only is it the code of the West, but it's the Christian thing to do.''

Susan nodded. They'd had no help growing up. But she had family and knew how family was. So, how bad could accepting help from his family be? Wasn't that what family was for?

# *Chapter Three*

It was easy to take frustrations out on family, Susan decided not an hour later as she listened to the brothers in the other room. "Why is Hawk so adamant about not accepting any help?" Susan asked Laura as they stood washing dishes with Zach's seventeen-year-old daughter, Angela.

Angela was the one who answered. With a roll of her eyes, she said, "Oh, that's just Uncle Jul. He hates his big brother to boss him around."

"I don't know Jul—Hawk very well," Laura said, shooting a warning look at Angela. "However, I would say Angela is partially right. Zach can be authoritative on occasion."

Angela giggled.

Laura shook her head and laid down the dish towel. "I suggest we go break it up before Zach and Julian end up hoarse. Angela, you finish loading the dishwasher. I'm sorry you missed dinner, Susan. You really should have joined us. You didn't have to eat out at the diner in town."

Susan shook her head. "I wanted to check on some things and didn't realize it'd gotten so late. I'm going to have to get used to how far it is into town. And to the next town, too."

Pushing through the swinging door, Susan entered the dining room. Zach and Julian sat at a dark wood table, both leaning forward as they argued back and forth.

"I told you earlier I don't require your help, Zach. I have everything under control."

"And I told you I thought it'd be a good idea to have some protection out there. That gang was only busted up a couple of months ago. We have no idea if everyone was caught. The investigation is still going on."

"We're a clinic, Zach. Besides, the trouble-makers probably fled the area when the DEA came down on them. No, you are not sending some of your men to live out there with us. If something comes up, I can reach Mitch by cell phone.''

"And what about Dr. Learner's reputation?'' Zach said.

Susan froze, halfway to the table, her eyes widening in shock.

Julian glanced at her, and the look of disbelief on his face hurt her female vanity. "Freckles? Oh, come on, she'll be my partner. There's nothing going on between us.''

Susan flushed. She wished the floor would open up and allow her to sink right through it.

"Oh? Well, maybe not, but what will people say?''

"I don't really—''

"We'll be hiring a receptionist who will also live in,'' Susan blurted out.

"What?'' both brothers said, turning their gaze to her.

Susan smiled weakly and shrugged her shoulders apologetically at Hawk, who stared with the same shocked expression as Zach—except that Zach relaxed as Hawk stiffened in disapproval. "I'm sorry, Hawk, that I haven't had a chance to talk to you about it. But while I was in town today, this older woman needed a job. She has typing skills and has a young son who is willing to work outside. Lita and Manuel. I hired them.''

"Without asking me?" Julian queried mildly, though his gaze darkened.

"She's your partner, isn't she?" Zach countered.

Laura rolled her eyes. "Did you two ever get along, Zach dear, or is this simply your way of communicating?"

Susan coughed into her hand. To see the woman take on her husband like that was enough to make the hardest of souls laugh. So quiet and easygoing, yet bluntly confronting such a big man. Susan didn't want anyone else to see her smile, but realized she'd failed miserably when Zach shot her a look of you-find-this-funny? Then he relaxed, a rueful smile appearing. "We're simply communicating, dear."

"So, is that why Hawk never hears me?" Susan asked, and moved over to the table, relieved Zach hadn't gotten upset at her amusement.

"I would have heard if you'd asked me about those two people," Julian muttered. "I don't mean to be disrespectful, but did you interview them before hiring them?"

Before Susan could answer, Zach said,

"Lita's a good egg. I don't remember her having a son, though."

Susan rested her elbows on the table, folding her hands. "Seems he's just arrived back in the area a year ago. Been working in a town north of here, but lost his job and needs another one badly. We could use a lot of work on the outside before winter and there are a lot of jobs inside we can get his help with. I thought it'd be worth hiring him. I called the hospital and got special permission for Lita to move in."

Julian sighed. "You should have checked with me first."

"Sorry. I'm just used to taking care of problems without asking." And she meant it. One of her major faults was doing first, asking later. "Should I call them up and tell them no?"

Julian looked at the woman sitting across from him. Her face glowed tonight, making the dark circles under her eyes much more evident. He hadn't seen them before. But if she had been back East lately, then she was still on that time zone, which meant it was very late to her. And he had been awfully hard on her today.

It was just such a shock to have her here. Of all the people who could have been assigned here with him, it had to be the very one who had driven him crazy during medical school and their internship—Freckles Learner.

Still, he hadn't been very professional with her, he realized. After all, she was a doctor, a professional, and deserved his respect. "No, Freckles. We can see how they work out. It's actually not a bad idea." Julian pushed back from the table. "I'm going for a walk. Laura, could you show Freckles, er, Dr. Learner where she'll be sleeping?"

"Sure." Laura stood also.

He should have known escaping unscathed was only a distant hope never to be fulfilled with Freckles Learner in the room. She jumped up, grinning, glowing. "Great. I'll go get my suitcase, and we can discuss this tomorrow, Hawk."

He saw it coming. The edge of the rug in the living room was flipped up. "Watch out!"

She tripped.

He jumped, grabbing at her.

She twisted.

Off balance and twisting again to catch her, he fell.

*Thud.*

"Oooaf." Julian couldn't help the groan as Freckles landed on him. When the stars faded, he focused and came nose-to-nose, eye-to-eye with the woman with whom he'd spent more time on the floor than any other person in his existence. Her eyes looked like saucers.

"Oh, no. I didn't see it. I can't believe..." She scrambled off him, leaving various spots that he was certain would be sore tomorrow.

"It's okay. At least you're okay." Zach reached out to steady Susan. Laura offered Julian a hand up. Julian waved her hand off, keeping his attention on Freckles. "You're just tired. Why don't you get some sleep?"

"How'd you know?" She actually looked surprised. Then she smiled, the gratitude lighting up her face like the morning sun touching the dew on rose petals. *Rose petals?* He shook his head. He must have hit it harder than he thought. "Thank you, Hawk." Her soft voice drew him back. "I am rather tired."

Julian heard Zach send Angela for the suitcase, and he watched as Laura led Susan off up the stairs.

"You okay, Jul?" Zach asked, walking over.

He forced his attention back to Zach and scowled at the speculative look on Zach's face. Julian rubbed his neck and groaned, realizing it was stiff. "I hate being near that woman. Every time I am she ends up in my arms and I end up on the ground," he growled.

"Do you really? Hate her, that is?" Zach asked mildly.

Julian's eyes nearly popped out of his head at Zach's words. He couldn't believe Zach actually thought he might be interested in Freckles. *Freckles.* How in the world could he be interested in her? She had red hair, green eyes, would probably burn in the sun out here and end up in the clinic—even though it was almost winter. Every single freckle on her face would disappear in a pool of red blistered skin, and those tiny hands of hers...

He thought about those tiny hands and what they'd probably look like after a month of working at such a rough clinic. Shaking his head, he silently admitted his brother's insinuations had him completely rattled. "You are definitely barking up the wrong tree there, big brother. She's dangerous. I have no desire to be near her. If I'd known she was going to be my partner I'd have taken an assignment in Outer Mongolia or somewhere."

"Mongolia is pretty remote." Zach chuckled.

"Exactly. She'd never find me. No, she probably would, and with my luck she'd have to examine a blow gun with curare in it and just happen to hit me. I swear, Zach, that woman…is… is…'' Julian shook his head and stalked outside.

Only when the screen closed a second time did he realize Zach had followed him.

"Tell me what's really bothering you, Hawk?"

"Don't call me that," he muttered.

Zach chuckled. "She likes the name."

"I know. And I did, until I heard her call me it."

"Why didn't you tell us about the nickname?"

Julian flushed. "Because."

"Oh, come on, Julian. Confess."

"You just can't let it go, can you?" Julian said, but there was no heat in his words. He loved his brothers deeply and never could stay angry with them. "In an experiment that our teacher purposely set up incorrectly, I was the only one who caught it—the only one ever to catch it in all of his classes. One of my friends was so wowed he started calling me Hawkeye. Eventually it was shortened to Hawk."

"I'm impressed."

Shaking his head, Julian said, "It was no big deal. If I had been paying attention and listening like everyone else I would have fallen for the bait he'd fed them. Instead, since I had no idea what was going on, I asked stupid questions that actually helped me out.''

''Funny way we get nicknames, isn't it?'' Zach patted him on the shoulder before slipping one of his booted feet up to the railing of the corral and staring off at the sky.

''It only reminds me to pay attention and do my best when I hear it.'' Julian crossed his arms over the corral bars. He gazed up at the dark night. The sound of crickets and the occasional buzzing insect filled the air. Wind, always wind, blew the grass and branches in one of their few trees. A horse made a noise in the distance and the sound of raised voices came from the nearby helpers' quarters. ''Freckles is the one who had distracted me that day. She was examining some of the chemical bottles that were set out on the table. I was just waiting for disaster to happen.''

''Ah, yes. Dr. Learner.'' Zach nodded. He shifted slightly, the fence creaking with his movement. A door in the distance slammed and then all was quiet again. ''She seems like a very nice, upbeat woman, although a tad clumsy.''

''Yeah, just a tad,'' Julian murmured dryly.

''She's certainly pretty,'' Zach observed.

"Maybe," Julian admitted reluctantly. He didn't like to examine that side of Freckles too closely. And he told Zach that. "I don't have time to notice things like that. I have a job to do."

"And then you're leaving?"

Julian wasn't surprised they were back to that. His brother didn't want him to leave. He wanted to keep control over all of them—and Julian wanted none of it. Carefully, he said, "I want to make something of myself."

"Julian." Zach sighed, and Julian could hear the disappointment in the way his older brother said his name.

Zach was good at acting like a parent. Having raised them, Zach did a lot of things most kids thought was reserved totally for parents, including the lectures.

"I've told you before, it's not what is on the outside, but what's in the heart that matters. When are you going to learn that? Your home, family, your relationship with God is what's important. Leaving here isn't going to solve your problem. Or release your guilt or pain or need to be away."

"And you only want to keep us all together," Julian put in.

Zach nodded. "True. Our roots are here. Hill Creek is our home. We need you here."

"And I just need time to learn what life is all about, Zach. I'm sorry you can't understand that."

Zach sighed. "I'm trying, Julian. I really am. I'll try to back off. But, Julian, know that I'm here, Mitch is here, if you need us."

Julian hesitated and then nodded before hugging his big brother. "I know that."

"And ask yourself why Freckles Learner drives you crazy every time you get within ten feet of her."

Julian turned to glare, but Zach was too fast. He'd already turned and started toward the house.

He knew why Freckles drove him crazy. She was a klutz. She just wasn't serious enough about her job. It wasn't that she threatened his need to go out and live life, since neither one of them had any desire to settle down and have a family. Not at all. No way. It was simply, he knew, if he was around her enough, he'd be the one who ended up injured from her accidents.

Self-preservation was all it was.

However, when the small voice within him asked *Preservation from what?* he couldn't answer.

# Chapter Four

"Now, just let me handle this. I know these people." Julian knew he was repeating himself, but he hadn't expected Susan to come along to the hospital planning commission's meeting.

Freckles looked good today. Of course, if Zach hadn't made a point of informing him just how nice-looking Freckles was, he probably never would have noticed. But now it seemed he couldn't take his eyes off her. As a woman, that was, not just as a threat to national security.

Julian couldn't ever remember seeing her in the conservative gray suit she wore that accented a smaller waist than he had realized she had. Yes, she was pleasantly plump, but it fit her perfectly. Not sickly skinny like the fashion models of today. Her hair was twisted up on the back of her head, emphasizing a gently curved jaw and high cheekbones. The freckles didn't seem so bright today, and it dawned on him she must be wearing makeup. A shame—the freckles made her look girlish in some way.

She carried a briefcase. It was the briefcase that made him nervous and kept his mind from being totally absorbed with how nice Susan looked. It swung next to her leg as she walked, back and forth, back and forth. Though not dangerous when most people carried one, it was easily a lethal weapon in her hands.

"You sure you don't want me to carry that briefcase for you?"

Susan shook her head, her eyes sparkling. "Really, Hawk, you act like I'm made of porcelain. I assure you, with four younger sisters and a younger brother, I'm a lot stronger than I look."

Julian had no doubt about that. He was the one who always ended up down for the count where this woman was concerned. Nevertheless, he nodded. "Okay, once again, this will be a short meeting for approval. Chuck has run this hospital for twenty years now. He's an intelligent man, good-natured and supportive. I'm sure it won't take long at all. He probably just wants to shoot the breeze over medical school, that sort of thing.''

"Ah, a good old boy," Susan murmured dryly. "I've met those before."

Julian shook his head. "No. He's not like that at all. He's a good man. You'll like him. He was supportive of my big brother after our parents died. If he hadn't backed Zach, I'm not sure we'd have gotten to stay together. I suppose you could say he's almost like a godparent.''

Susan smiled her apology for misunderstanding Julian.

Julian accepted it with a nod of his own.

"I knew someone like him a long time ago. We called him 'old Sam.'''

Those words caught Julian's attention. "You called him? What do you mean? That wasn't his name?''

Turning down the white sterile hall, Julian touched Susan's elbow as they came upon a bump in the tiles of the floor. All kinds of imagery filled his mind as he approached the fold, all showing some kind of detriment to his health.

She didn't trip, to his great relief, nor did the

briefcase leave any lasting bruises on his body. He breathed a silent sigh of relief.

"I don't know what his real name was. He lived downstairs from us." Susan's eyes were unfocused for a moment and she smiled. "He was a good man," she said, repeating his own words back to him. "He was always bringing us home treats, helping me with the younger kids when I was trying to get them to the bus stop, little things like that."

"You miss him?" Julian queried, able to tell by the tone of her voice that this man had indeed been someone special in her life.

"He's dead," she replied, her gaze returning to the present, just in time to avoid a potted plant. "He was caught in gang cross fire one day," she said matter-of-factly. "I have the reassurance he's with God, though."

Julian felt the shock down to his toes. *Gang cross fire?*

"He's the one who brought us to the knowledge of Jesus Christ."

Before he could pursue what she'd said, they arrived at their destination. Julian made a note to ask more about the story later.

Julian breathed a quiet prayer asking God to guide them and then pushed the door open. He stepped back, allowing Susan entrance before going in himself.

Smiling, Julian nodded at Tilda, who sat at the secretary's desk. Her sturdy wood desk was cluttered with papers and miscellaneous office supplies. The only thing breaking the monotony of the desk was a picture of Tilda's grandkids and a small bud vase with a carnation in it. Tilda had been with the hospital as long as he could remember. Every Friday night she went to the movie theater. Every Sunday afternoon over to her daughter's. And once a month when he was a kid she would stop by his house and drop off "just something extra" she'd cooked. She was a good woman, Julian thought. "Morning, Tilda," he greeted. "We're here to see Chuck."

Lifting her hands from the keyboard, the gray-haired woman smiled warmly. "He and the others are in there." She motioned back toward Chuck's office.

"The others?" Julian questioned, confused.

Tilda's smile turned sympathetic. "You've got some opposition, Doctor."

Susan touched his elbow, and he glanced around at her.

"Let's go." She looked as if she expected trouble.

Julian knew better. "Don't worry. We have contracts. I'm sure there's just some misunderstanding."

"You are a very trusting person, Hawk," Susan murmured.

*Not really,* he thought. Still, he'd come too far to lose his dream of getting out of this town in two years instead of five. He wasn't going to forfeit it now simply because of some sudden opposition. Everything would be just fine.

He kept telling himself that as he walked down the short hall to the meeting room off Chuck's office.

Pushing open the door, he stepped onto the plush mauve carpet and came face-to-face with his opposition.

Bate Masterson stared coldly at them as they entered.

Turning his gaze from the man who hated all McCades, Julian located Chuck and nodded. "Good morning, Dr. Gonzalez." Abruptly he said, "Mr. Masterson."

"Come in. Have a seat, Julian, Susan. Good to see you again, Susan."

Julian slipped a hand to the small of Susan's back, feeling overly protective of her. Perhaps it was the look in Bate's eyes, the look of wanting to devour them. Julian didn't know and at this point didn't care. He silently berated himself for bringing Susan into a potentially volatile situation.

Julian decided to get right to the point. "What's up, Chuck?"

Chuck seated himself at the mahogany table. Julian pulled out a chair for Susan, watching as she set her briefcase on the table in front of her before dropping gracefully into the plush cushioned chair. He seated himself next to her and accepted the cup of coffee offered him, though he didn't drink it. He was afraid to pick it up and have it end up in his lap if Susan made some quick move. Moving it to his far right side, outside Susan's range, he waited for Chuck to speak.

Chuck shuffled through a stack of papers before passing them across the table to Susan and Julian. "It seems the board, represented by Bate here, took a vote and decided that a clinic just might not be the best thing right now."

Stunned, Julian simply stared. "You can't be serious."

"Excuse me?" Susan said, her own voice betraying her surprise.

Bate smiled apologetically. "We felt, since

Dr. Morrison abandoned that old clinic and moved it to his house on the edge of town, he must have had good reasons. It is known that he lost patients out there years ago. If I'm not mistaken, that's why he moved closer to town.''

"Old Doc Morrison was lazy and didn't want to live out there. And even if that wasn't the case, medicine is vastly different from twenty years ago.''

Julian shook with anger. Taking a breath, he worked to calm himself, then took a quick moment to glance at Susan to see how she was taking this. It certainly surprised him to see a calm, steady, quiet demeanor about her.

"Be that as it may,'' Bate said coldly, "the board has decided it'd be safer simply to forget that idea and just move you to the hospital for the next five years under close supervision.''

"But we're not interns!'' Julian said, losing his cool.

Chuck opened his mouth to calm Julian, but didn't get the chance. Susan spoke, her quiet, sure voice cutting through the anger and tension with soothing effect. "Can you explain, please, how you plan to break these contracts without this entire hospital closing down because of the lawsuit one of us might file for breach of contract?''

Julian had to blink and look again to make sure this was the same klutzy woman he knew. *Breach of contract?* The meek, mild woman who somehow had gotten through medical school had just challenged Bate Masterson and Chuck Gonzales.

Bate spluttered. ''Now, just a minute, missy. Those words could be taken harshly. Why don't you just leave this to the rest of us here?''

Chuck's mouth quirked up in a grin before he covered it with a hand, coughing instead.

Julian did a slow burn at Bate's words. ''Dr. Learner is just as qualified to state how she feels about her contract being broken as I am. Let's not exclude her.''

He couldn't believe he'd just said that. Only moments ago, he'd told her to let him handle everything. But Bate's demeaning words, aimed to humiliate Susan, had angered him. He turned to see what would come out of Susan's mouth next—and watched when she handed a set of folders across the table for Bate to examine.

Bate and Chuck took the papers and scanned them. So did Julian. He was stunned to find a financial report on the hospital over the past six months. How had she gotten all this information? And better yet, why? He hadn't expected trouble. She must have been anticipating something like this.

Bate's scowl turned black and he glared at them, malevolence in his eyes. "This won't work."

Julian simply stared at Bate. "Take it back to the board and ask them. A contract is a contract, Mr. Masterson. Will any industry, any groups, ever trust your word again if we take you to court over the fact that you broke a contract with us simply because you decided it'd be more convenient to have us at the hospital? It's not like we've broken rules, proved ourselves unable to handle the situation or ended up in a dangerous situation that might compromise the hospital."

Bate threw his papers down onto the table and stood. "You aren't going anywhere. It would have gone a lot easier on you if you'd cooperated."

Julian wanted to ask why. Susan's voice stopped him. "For whom, Mr. Masterson? The sick people who can't make it to the hospital and receive proper medical care, or the board?"

"You have no idea what you're talking about. Well, we'll see how long you last. Go on, go out there, go play country doctor. But don't expect us to honor the same contract when you come begging. You won't find a job at this hospital waiting for you.''

He stormed out. Julian watched him, wondering just what he'd done to convince the board members to vote against the clinic, and what he would do to put further roadblocks in their path.

''I'm sorry about that, Julian, Susan. We're run by a board and my hands were basically tied.'' Chuck offered the apology with sincerity.

Julian shook his head. ''That's just Masterson.''

''Did he mean his threat?'' Susan asked.

Chuck nodded wearily and leaned back in his chair. ''I'm certain he did. He's been against the clinic reopening since they were told Julian would be the doctor to replace old Doc Morrison. Didn't like it one bit. Now that he's gotten the other board members to vote against you on the clinic, he'll keep a close watch on you. First mistake you make and those contracts can be canceled. It won't take anything to convince the board not to allow you on staff. And in your case, Julian, I happen to know you took out a personal loan to help get your business started out there at the clinic. That'd probably be called in early if you lost your job.''

Julian scowled.

Susan glanced at Dr. Gonzales, bewildered but nodding. ''I see.'' Turning to Julian, she attempted a smile. ''At least we still have our jobs as of this minute—and aren't being shuffled back into the hospital like interns.''

Julian nodded. Pushing back he stood and held out a hand to Chuck Gonzales. ''Thank you for seeing us, Chuck. About that equipment we needed...''

Chuck smiled slyly. ''Well, seeing as how the clinic is still open, it would be bad publicity for the hospital to renege on its responsibility of outfitting the clinic now, wouldn't it?'' He winked at Susan.

Susan chuckled and stood. ''You're right, Dr. Gonzales, it would.''

''I do wish you hadn't spent so much of your money on other items and had waited.''

''I needed that equipment and the hospital wasn't going to supply it. You know that.''

''Hmm,'' the doctor suddenly said. ''Maybe we can convince the board to pick up those costs.''

Smiling, Julian shook his hand. ''I can imagine Bate's response. No, I don't think so. Thanks anyway.''

Julian reached for Susan's briefcase at the same time she did.

Hands met. Julian swore if he hadn't been distracted by the surge of unaccountable awareness that swept through him, he would have seen it coming. But he didn't.

Too stunned by the shock of concentrating on the soft smooth skin of the tiny hand he'd accidentally grabbed with the briefcase handle, he didn't notice her jerk back. He only felt a tug and then she fell forward, overbalanced.

Eyes widening, he let go of the briefcase and grabbed for her.

He, Susan and the briefcase went down in a pile.

And once again, Julian felt pain radiating out in all directions.

The briefcase had done its damage after all.

Julian realized the next two years were going to be a very long, painful two years with Freckles Learner at his side.

# *Chapter Five*

"Can we stop at the café? I'm starving."

Susan didn't want to be locked up in a car just yet with Julian on the long ride back. He was still walking funny. And as long as he was still in pain, she was afraid he'd be grouchy. Oh, why had he grabbed her briefcase like that? Susan silently moaned all over again. Only around this man did bad things happen. Just him. No one else.

Julian smiled a bit painfully. "Sure. I'm a bit hungry, too. And it might be a good time to discuss the clinic."

Relieved, Susan smiled.

Julian turned his car down the main street and

pulled into a parking space next to the curb. Opening her own door, Susan slid out of the car and joined Julian on the sidewalk. "So, what exactly happened back there, Hawk?" she queried as they started down the sidewalk past the mercantile store toward the local café.

"What do you mean?"

"With that Masterson person. I sensed he definitely wanted to upset you."

Julian nodded at someone who called out a greeting as he continued down the sidewalk. "He doesn't really like our family. His family was one of the founding fathers of Hill Creek. His dad didn't get along with my mom and dad. Evidently, my parents bought a major portion of their land when the Mastersons were having financial problems. Bate Masterson became bitter at my parents after his dad died. He wasn't satisfied with his inheritance. He is rich, but still dissatisfied, wanting more," Julian said, his voice reflecting his frustration. "It has only intensified over the years. Things really got bad when his son ran for sheriff and my brother Mitch won."

Julian pulled open the door and escorted Susan inside. Susan couldn't help but enjoy the fact that she and Hawk were going to share a meal together, alone, just the two of them. So many years of dozens around and no time to date. She had never been out on an official date. Nor was this. But she was with a man she found attractive, a good man who cared, who was gentle, kind and compassionate.

"Well, no Mitch in here," Julian murmured, and Susan looked around, noting his brother wasn't in evidence. Silently, she admitted Hawk was a bit absorbed in getting away from his family.

She had wanted to escape her own family at one time and had found out very quickly how much she missed them. She had prayed, though, and believed this was God's will, to come out here to this job, to help start up this clinic. Soon she'd see her family again. She had to trust God's wisdom and just push the feelings of missing her family aside.

"I like Mitch," Susan murmured to Julian as she slid into a booth.

"So do I," Julian said, and dropped into the seat across from her. "I just don't want to discuss the meeting with him right now."

He signaled a young dark-haired Hispanic woman, who came over to the table. "Hi, Suzi."

"Welcome home, Julian." The woman, perhaps in her mid-twenties, smiled, her eyes twinkling. "What can I get for you today?"

Julian looked at Susan. "You know what you want?"

Actually, she didn't. "Do you have salad?"

Julian shook his head. "Dinner salads," he said before Suzi could answer. "Bring us both the lunch special, Suzi, and two teas and water."

"Will do...Hawk," she said as she started off toward the counter.

Julian groaned.

"She called you Hawk. I didn't know anyone else knew that nickname around here."

Julian met Susan's gaze. "She knows Mitch, and it looks like Mitch has been talking."

Susan chuckled. "It's not so bad. Nicknames can be good."

"You might feel differently if you had one growing up."

"You had one growing up?" Susan asked.

Julian shrugged. "Dumpy, bumponalog, Jul, to name a few."

"Dumpy? What in the world did that mean?"

Julian scowled. "I was a chunky baby, evidently. How about you? Did you have any nicknames?"

Susan smiled, thinking back on her brother and sisters. "Yeah. I was Sissy."

"Ah, well, that's not too bad."

"I didn't say it was bad. However, my brother and sisters did have nicknames ranging from Sugar Pie to Baby Bear, among the nicer ones."

"Zach never had nicknames. The luck of being the oldest, I suppose."

Suzi returned. "Here you go. Two hamburger plates." Setting down the tray, she handed them their food and drinks. "Call if you need anything."

Susan murmured her thanks along with Julian and then picked up a knife to cut her hamburger in half.

Julian picked his up and took a bite out of it.

"Getting back to our conversation earlier, didn't Bate know you had a contract with the hospital?"

She picked up a piece of her burger and took a bite.

"Oh, yeah. I don't think he really believed I could make the grades. I was always right on the line. I didn't care much for school, until I decided to be a doctor. I really think he thought I'd either drop out or come back to the hospital where I'd be under some doctor that was one of his cronies. He doesn't like it one bit that Chuck runs the outreach centers and will be the one responsible for the clinics.''

Susan swallowed and sipped her tea.

''Speaking of which,'' Julian continued, ''how did you know we were going to have trouble?''

''I didn't,'' Susan replied, polishing off another bite of food. Patting her mouth with her napkin, she continued, ''However, I have learned that if it can go wrong, it usually does and it's better to always be prepared just in case. Before I took the job at the clinic I wanted to make sure such an out-of-the-way hospital could really pay me. I researched them, checked out newspaper articles about the hospital and even found some mention of the interest in reopening the clinic. I heard they had one nearby, on the other side of the next town. I guess that's one of Dr. Gonzales's, too. But they are taken to a different hospital, aren't they? Anyway, it didn't cost me much at all to hire someone to gather that information for me. It's all in my briefcase—an analysis of the hospital and its financial status. I also have a projected summary of their status over the next two years. Did you know they're expecting people to be moving out this way and that this area will grow?''

She could tell she'd surprised Julian. ''No, I didn't.''

''Those are just the forecasts. At any rate, I knew there was a clinic. I didn't realize it was in this bad a shape, though. Well, I didn't tell the person who did the clipping for me to find out too much about the clinic, so it's my own fault.''

''I'd say you were much more prepared than I was,'' he said, slightly downcast.

*Uh-oh.* Susan had heard those words from her siblings before in just that voice. ''Not really, Hawk,'' she soothed. ''You come from this area. You know the people and know things I would never know,'' she continued, trying to boost him. ''I simply knew the facts. You have just spent the last twenty-five minutes telling me about the two people we met. Had you not been there, I would never have guessed Dr. Gonzales was on our side in this. He was so quiet and withdrawn.''

''He's a very quiet man.''

Susan watched him carefully, worried she had hurt his feelings. She was relieved when his mouth quirked.

"I'm okay, Susan. Stop staring at me like I'm going to bite your head off. My poor bruised ego will survive."

His eyes twinkled, and she realized he'd read right through her attempts to make him feel better. She felt herself blush.

His eyes focused on her cheeks and his smile turned warm, his gaze interested. At least, she was almost certain that was what she saw.

Abruptly he slid out of the booth and stood. "I'll be right back. Excuse me, Susan."

She blinked in surprise as he turned and strode off toward the bathroom. Suzi came back and cleared away the dishes, bringing her a cup of hot tea. And still Susan sat there staring after where Julian had disappeared.

Had she misread him and embarrassed him somehow? She really wished she understood the emotions that were churning around inside her—and him—better than she did. She could talk to him as she would her siblings, but perhaps she had said something or done something that she just shouldn't do when talking with someone of the opposite sex who she was interested in. *Father, guide me. I'm attracted to this man even though I know I really don't have time to be distracted from my job. But he's nice, funny and*

*wonderful. If this isn't Your will, open my eyes
to my folly.*

A memory verse from Sunday school reminded her that God was in control in all things, and so she let go of her worry and gave her insecurities to God.

The bell over the front door jingled, and Susan saw three men come in. They were laughing. Two of the men faded into the background compared to the third one. She'd seen his type before. She recognized it from the streets. Cocky, arrogant, owning the world. They were all the same. Bullies, pure and simple. She wondered who this one was.

His gaze met hers and then traveled over her. Susan remained passive, knowing he was assessing her as any bully would. He started down the aisle, pausing to call out an order to Suzi, who stiffened before moving to obey. That confirmed what she'd sensed upon his entering. She would never forget that kind of attitude.

"Hi there, sugar. And what's your name?" the sandy-haired young man asked as he swaggered over. The two other men took up stations in the aisle while this one made himself at home by sliding into Julian's seat.

Susan picked up her cup and took a sip of tea,

watching the irritation flare in the man's eyes when she didn't answer immediately. Setting her cup down, she finally said, "Dr. Learner. And if you'll excuse me, I'm just finishing up here and leaving."

She moved to get up. The tall, skinny cowboy who had come in with his boss didn't move but stared at the leader instead. Mr. Congeniality shook his head slightly, indicating his cohort should stay put.

Turning his attention back to her, he smiled a really syrupy smile. "Now, that's not very friendly of you. Maybe it's because you're new you don't understand the code out here. You might ask me to have a seat—"

"You're already seated," she replied.

He chuckled. "And then we'd share lunch and get to know each other better."

The short, wiry cowboy who blocked the aisle with his tall friend snickered.

"And here I thought the West was known for its friendliness. My mistake. I've seen better manners from a warthog. Now, excuse me, please," she repeated and stood, forcing the man away from her by the simple act of standing. He had to either move or force her back into her seat. She was betting that in a café full of people, he wouldn't do that.

He didn't. But the other one didn't appreciate it, either. He stood and grabbed her arm before she could shove past. "Just a minute," he started.

"Back off, Noble." Julian came strolling down the aisle, his eyes shooting fire.

"What's the matter, Juls? You upset 'cause I'm staking a claim?"

Susan rolled her eyes. "No one is staking a claim. But I'd suggest you get your hand off me right now unless you want me to press charges— or worse, tick me off and then come in for medical treatment when I'm on call."

Noble's eyes burned with anger, and he increased the pressure on her arm. The only thing that kept her from crying out in pain was the fact that she knew he wanted her to do just this.

Then Julian was by her side and Noble released her. "Come on, Susan. Let's go."

"I'd like to say it's been a pleasure," Susan murmured as they passed Noble and his two men. She didn't finish the sentence, but instead allowed Julian to guide her out of the restaurant. She winced when she heard a vile curse hurled after her.

Julian stiffened and started to turn. "No, Julian. Words can't hurt."

Julian hesitated and then nodded. "You're right. I'm sorry I left you and allowed that *person* near you."

"Ah, so you know him, do you?" Susan chuckled.

"That's Bate's son. His father may despise us and work to quietly erode our reputation, but Noble isn't as subtle. He is very blatant about hating us."

"I just don't understand hate like that," she murmured. "I've seen it a lot, though."

"I guess it depends on each situation. I even know some Christians who are like that. They won't open up and let God heal their heart. Maybe they don't know how. The more they hurt, the angrier they get."

"I don't think that family was very nice to begin with," Susan murmured as she turned the corner.

"Not really. They've always been very superior about just who they were and what they owned. Nothing I can do about the past. Just have to concentrate on the present. And the best way to handle that family is not to deal with them unless it's necessary. Nothing Zach ever did pleased them, and he did try. Finally had to give it over to God.''

Arriving at Julian's car, he slipped the key into the lock and turned before pulling the door open for Susan. ''Susan,'' he said, stopping her from getting in simply by laying his hand on her arm.

Unconsciously she winced.

Julian paused, looking at her quizzically. ''What's the matter?''

''Nothing. I'm fine.'' She knew he read the lie in her eyes. His deep, penetrating stare searched out and found the truth without another word.

''Take off your jacket.''

Susan shook her head, embarrassed. ''I'm fine, Hawk. Really.''

He moved up closer, trapping her against the back of the car. ''Noble hurt your arm, didn't he?''

His fingers went to the buttons of her jacket and slipped them loose before his hands slid up inside the jacket and eased it off her shoulders. His touch was warm, gentle and so very coaxing she couldn't argue. ''Only a bit. I bruise easily, Hawk.''

He didn't listen, but pushed her jacket off the

one arm and reached for the cuff of her long-sleeved top. Slipping the button, he eased it up. Susan was shocked to see the outline of finger-prints. What shocked her even more was Julian's reaction. He trembled. Touching the bruises, outlining them with his index finger, he actually trembled as his features darkened. "You have no idea what I'd like to do to that jerk right now."

Susan put a hand over Julian's to draw his attention away from the bruises.

He glanced at her.

She used that distraction to push her shirt-sleeve down.

Julian reached for the sleeve to push it back up, and she touched his hand again. He hesitated before capturing her hand in his.

"Don't allow Noble's stupid actions to push you into something. Just let it go."

Julian tightened his hand on hers. "He hurt you, Susan, simply because he was angry at me."

Susan chuckled. "Not quite. I turned down getting to know him better. It hurt his ego."

"That doesn't give him the right to do this."

"No, it doesn't. Nothing gives him the right to do this. However, I'm not worried about it. I think the best way to handle this is not at all. If I go running to tell someone, he's going to see it as a victory of getting to me. So I am going to ignore it. I'd ask you ignore it, too.''

Julian hesitated.

"Hey, Jul, I thought our big brother taught you better than this.''

Susan heard the amusement and glanced over to see Mitch ambling toward them. "Hello, Sheriff.'' Susan offered him a tentative smile, wondering if he had overheard something.

"Hello, brother.'' Julian's voice was not welcoming at all. Mitch's smile only broadened at his tone.

"Problem here?'' he asked as he stopped near them, his gaze going from one to the other, scrutinizing the way her jacket hung loosely on her, one sleeve unbuttoned.

Susan looked at Julian, silently begging him not to tell even as she reddened under Mitch's gaze.

Julian hesitated and then shook his head. "Just helping Dr. Learner with her jacket.''

Relieved, she smiled gratefully and willingly turned as he stepped back and helped her into her jacket.

She could see the suspicion on Mitch's features, but he didn't pursue it. Instead, he pursued something else. "So how'd the meeting go?"

Susan turned and murmured her thanks to Julian.

"Bate tried to stop the clinic from opening."

Mitch scowled. "You already have a contract. He can't do that."

Julian grinned. "As Susan informed him. I think she changed his mind."

Mitch turned and studied Susan more closely before grinning. "Good for you."

Susan accepted the praise. "I had no idea I'd be walking into a family feud here," she offered.

Mitch shook his head. "They're bad news all around. Stay away from them, Dr. Learner. If you have problems, come to me."

"Thank you, Sheriff."

"Call me Mitch."

"Mitch," she corrected.

"Now if you'll excuse us," Julian interrupted and again opened the door for Susan.

He saw the surprise in Susan's gaze and the knowing look in Mitch's. He ignored them both. Closing the door behind Susan, he walked around the car. "See you at supper, I'd be willing to bet," Julian said.

Mitch grinned. "I never was a betting man."

Julian shook his head and slid into the car.

"What was that all about, Hawk?" Susan asked.

He heard the bewilderment in her voice at his abruptness. "Just Mitch. I didn't want to get into another discussion about the Mastersons on the street. Mitch is a sheriff and has to be impartial. It's hard to do when it comes to them. No reason to add fuel to the fire."

"Ah. I imagine that's hard for him. I'd never thought about the position an officer might be in if they knew the person."

"It's different here in such a small town. In a bigger city it's a lot less likely to happen. But here, everyone knows everyone. That is both good and bad."

Susan pulled her briefcase onto her lap and started rummaging through it, falling silent.

Julian pulled out and headed back to the ranch. The workers were at the clinic and the basics were being done. There wasn't much else they could do today.

What had gotten into him back at the café? He'd actually flirted with Freckles. Freckles Learner. The bane of his existence. Had he missed that much sleep? He wasn't attracted to the woman. He couldn't even be around her for more than thirty minutes before she injured him. He was still sore from the briefcase incident earlier. He had to be out of his mind.

He knew!

His brother's words had warped him. He hadn't shown any interest in anyone since returning to Hill Creek. Having his big brother point out how attractive Freckles was had simply drawn his attention to it. Because of that, he naturally had forgotten everything that had happened before and was looking at her simply as a woman, not as a danger to his life.

Forget the silly grin of hers or the way she blushed so prettily when he teased her. Nor did he want to remember the way her gaze had softened when she'd returned his smile. That smile of hers had curled his toes in his shoes. As had the loose strand of hair hanging against her cheek, resting there so lazily...or the simple way she had been so polite and nice to Suzi when many hadn't been. Of course, she didn't know Suzi had an illegitimate daughter. It drove him crazy to see the way people sneered at her.

Small-town gossip.

And now he had probably put Freckles right in the middle of it after that scene at the café. Noble was bad news. Julian had gone to the bathroom simply to get away from Freckles and regain his perspective. He'd come back to find Noble harassing her, and his protective instincts had gone on full alert.

That and the fact he wanted Noble to have nothing to do with her.

Shaking his head, he let it go for now and simply drove.

"Here you go," Susan said, her soft voice breaking the silence in the car. "Here's the report the agency got together for me."

Julian accepted the manila folder. "You don't have to give me a copy, Freckles—"

"Of course I do. We'll be partners at this clinic. You should know everything going on financially with the hospital, just like I should. Especially since we're only an outreach. Under the indirect supervision of Dr. Gonzales."

"Yeah. Well, since I now own the building and they own the equipment, this should prove interesting."

"You bought the building?" Surprise colored Susan's voice.

"Seemed like the best thing to do. They didn't have an official clinic set up yet. I borrowed the money and bought the old clinic, then approached the hospital about opening up a clinic. They're renting the building from me. They are providing the bigger equipment, while I have purchased what I can of the smaller equipment.''

''So, in essence, they're paying you for the building and you get to do what you want, which is work in a clinic? Why did they want a second doctor?''

''Don't get me wrong, Susan. This is their clinic. They're the ones who originally agreed to open it. At the time they still had one open. Of course, it was out of Doc Morrison's house. I guess they didn't think of moving it, or didn't realize Chuck and I had discussed it. He and I both believe it's a good idea to have one out where the people are.''

''But why buy the building?''

''An investment. When I move on, I'll still be receiving revenue. And if something happens, I can always rent out the space to other doctors.''

Susan nodded, impressed.

There were some risks and problems, but he had other plans made as well to cover those. It was only one more small step to prove to his brothers he could make it on his own.

''So why do you want to work out here?'' he

asked Susan. "Why'd you take Dr. Gonzales up on his offer?"

He waited for her answer, and it was slow in coming. Finally she said, "I had bills to pay off and I'm putting money away into an account for future college bills."

Future college bills? Now, there was one Julian hadn't heard before. Susan certainly enjoyed learning if she planned to continue in college. She was very frugal, too, he noted.

Turning onto their land, he allowed the silence to go on as she dug some more in her briefcase and rearranged things.

When they pulled up to the ranch, Susan climbed out and headed toward the house. Julian wasn't far behind her. He wanted to change and go for a ride, get away for a while, contemplate everything that had happened today and hopefully get his odd feelings back under control and his priorities right. After all, his job came first, and with that job his responsibility to make sure Freckles Learner didn't plague his patients with the disasters she so frequently plagued him with.

With that in mind, he walked on into the house.

# *Chapter Six*

"**D**id you see Laura outside, Miss Susan?"

Susan, in her new jeans and tennis shoes, paused by the kitchen door to smile at Angela. "Hello. I think I saw her out near the corral."

Angela giggled. "Laura spends all of the time she's not on duty out there by the horses."

"I was just going out there. Want to walk with me?" Susan offered. She liked Angela. She reminded her a lot of Chrissy, her younger sister back East.

"Yeah. I'm done here, and I want to go visit a friend. Guess what?" she continued, going out the door. "I have my learner's permit and will get my full license in just two more months."

"Really?" Susan asked, walking alongside Angela.

"Yeah. I already run errands for Daddy around the ranch, but I can't go into town, especially since my uncle is the sheriff. I'd get a ticket. But soon I'll be able to." Angela's step was light as she led Susan across the yard.

Walking up to the corral, Susan watched as Laura worked with a horse.

"That's Jingle Bells. Laura's adopted her, though Jingle Bells hasn't really adopted my stepmom. Well, maybe she has," Angela said, and climbed up on the fence. "Jingle Bells doesn't really want me riding her anymore. She only likes Laura to ride her."

Laura lost her seat and fell hard in the straw.

"You can't tell it," Susan murmured.

"They're just in a struggle of superiority right now. When Jingle Bells accepts Laura isn't going to give in, she'll stop tossing Laura."

Laura sat up, grabbed the reins, got nose-to-nose with the horse and muttered something to the animal before crawling back up on Jingle Bells. Again they went through the routine. This time, however, Laura was ready and didn't allow the horse to dump her when it dropped its head.

When it acted as if it was going to roll, Laura pulled hard on the reins.

"Nice horse," Susan whispered.

"Ever ridden?" Angela asked.

"Nope," Susan replied.

Laura danced around the yard with the horse until it started walking the way she directed it. Then she hopped off, praised the horse and finally headed to where Angela was standing. Wiping a hand over her forehead, she chuckled. "That horse puts me through the same routine every day. When is she going to learn?"

"When you stop giving in and letting her get away with it," Angela said, grinning. "Guess what? Susan has never ridden a horse before. Can you believe that?"

Laura rolled her eyes at Susan. "Out here that's considered a sin."

"Uh-oh," Susan said, looking at Angela. "Let me guess, you want to teach me?"

"Nah, I'll let Uncle Jul do that. He rides really good. I have decided I won't be a horse trainer when I grow up, just a vet. I'll leave the training to someone who can. Maybe then they'll learn to ride faster than my stepmom did."

Laura reached out and ran a hand through Angela's hair. "You did fine. It's this stubborn horse with the weird sense of humor that thwarted you.''

"What is it you'll let me do, Angie?'' Julian asked, walking up.

"Susan needs to learn how to ride. I told her you'd help.''

Susan turned, and her breath stopped. Julian in a suit or dress pants was quite a sight, but Julian in jeans, boots, blue shirt and cowboy hat was a knockout. She simply stared. She couldn't help it. He didn't look at all the way she'd seen him before.

She watched him pull on his jean jacket and push his hat back. "I was going riding....''

When he hesitated, Susan flushed. "It's all right. I really have no desire to be on a horse.''

"But Uncle Jul, you have to teach her. What if an emergency happens and she needs to go somewhere and all the vehicles are tied up? She'd have to go to Uncle Mitch's, and she couldn't get there without a horse. Or maybe she had to come out and find you for a medical emergency. Or what if—''

"Okay, okay, Angie!'' Julian said, chuckling. "Come on, Susan. It's imperative I teach you right now in case an emergency comes up while I'm gone.''

He rolled his eyes and winked at Susan as he took her arm and led her off toward the barn. She could hear Laura say something to Angela and Angela replying, but not what was said. She was too embarrassed to concentrate on a conversation. "Really, Hawk. If you want to go riding, you don't have to teach me anything right now."

Hawk grinned. "Oh, I'm going riding. You can go along with me. That'll be your lesson. And we'll be out of Angela's reach."

Susan shook her head. "Shame on you," she whispered to him.

"Do you really want to spend the next hour with pip-squeak there telling you what you're doing wrong?"

"Not really. But she said—"

"—that I'd teach you. Yeah. But she wouldn't be able to resist helping. Believe me. Come on."

Julian went into the barn and quickly saddled two horses. "Now, up we go." He took her foot and placed it in the stirrup and then boosted her up, helping her with her other leg. "Let me check the length of the stirrups. Stand up." He measured the room between her bottom and the saddle. "Okay, sit. Hold these until I'm mounted." He tossed her the reins.

He quickly mounted his own horse and moved over by her, taking the reins from her. "Hold on to the saddle horn. Here we go."

"You know, Hawk, I really don't know if this is such a go-ooo-oo—"

The rest was cut off as he turned and started the horses out of the barn. She felt every bounce slap her bottom and jar her teeth. Vaguely she heard Angela shout and Laura exclaim, but she was too busy trying to keep from biting her tongue in half to comment.

"Move with the horse, Susan, like this," he said. She watched but couldn't figure out what he was doing differently than her, except talking and keeping all his teeth in one place. She was certain hers were going to bounce right out of her head.

"No, no. Like this," he said. He stopped their horses by a gate and showed her before climbing down and pulling the gate open.

She tried to imitate his motions.

He climbed back up on the horse and they were off again. Step *smack* step *smack* step *smack*...

Susan groaned in time to the smacks until

slowly she realized every step wasn't followed with a smack of her bottom and a click of her teeth.

The barn was out of sight, though, by that time and Susan was certain her eyeballs were permanently bugged out from the pressure of trying to stay on the horse.

"There you go. You're getting it. Now let's speed it up."

And they were off. Susan couldn't hold back a scream as they went along at such a fast pace. She'd just conquered one thing, thought she'd done well, and now here she was, being shown what real riding was all about. *Father, don't let me die. Let me live so I can kill him first,* she prayed irreverently. *Okay, okay, maybe not kill him, but let him have it with both barrels...okay, not both barrels, but plan a good revenge.*

Susan kept plotting and planning as they rode along. It was the only thing that kept her going as Hawk shouted and pointed out landmarks as they went. When they came to a small creek, he finally pulled up.

Julian swung down off his horse and stretched. "That felt wonderful. How about you?" He smiled and headed back to her horse.

"I don't know," she said through clenched teeth. "Feeling left about thirty minutes ago."

Julian frowned. "I'm sorry, Freckles. I didn't think." Reaching up, he slid his hands around her waist and pulled her down, toward him.

Susan couldn't stop herself as she fell into him.

Thankfully, he was ready for that and caught her up against his chest. "Just take it easy. Can you stand on your legs at all?"

The concern in his voice melted her anger away. He truly hadn't realized what he was doing. "No," she whispered, her arms clinging around his neck. "I was serious when I said I couldn't feel them."

"You should have said something, Freckles," he murmured. Turning slightly, he bent and then lifted her in his arms. "I didn't think. I know you're in shape, but you haven't ridden horses before. This is my fault."

Moving over, he sat her down on a limb hanging from a tree that had lost most of its leaves by now. "Just a minute."

He hurried over, tied up the horses and returned.

Susan winced when she moved. Julian was all

professional as he hunkered down in front of her. "Tell me where you hurt, Freckles."

"Gluteus muscles and on down to my knees. Even my lower lumbar region."

Julian reached out and poked gently but firmly on her back. "Here? And here?" he said, taking her moans as a yes.

"Oh, Freckles, I am so sorry. You're going to be really sore tomorrow, I'm afraid."

Susan winced. "Thanks for the warning."

"Why didn't you just use common sense and stop before you were in pain?"

"Why didn't you use common sense and not push me when I was in pain?"

"Yeah, that's the question, isn't it?"

The disgust in his voice made her wonder why he hadn't thought to ask her in the first place and just what he was thinking to make him sound so upset suddenly.

"We should walk," he said. "It might work some of the soreness out. And if you don't move around, you'll really regret it tomorrow."

She stared into his eyes and he returned her stare.

What was that she suddenly saw in those eyes? Tenderness, caring and concern. "You'll make a wonderful doctor, Hawk,'' she whispered.

"Thanks, Freckles," he returned.

The neighing of a horse broke the moment, and they turned to see Angela riding up in the distance. Susan wasn't sure if she was happy or sad to see Angela. Teenagers had the worst timing sometimes. Still, she and Julian had passed some point just now. She'd seen it in his eyes. There was no wariness there, but acceptance. Did that possibly mean he realized not everyone was perfect?

"My niece arrives. Come on, Freckles, up we go. Time to walk."

Susan groaned but rose. "I am really going to get you for this, do you know that, Hawk?"

Julian chuckled. "Promises, promises. You're too nice to stoop to revenge."

He slipped his arm around her and started walking, holding her up against his side.

"We'll see, Hawk. Just wait and we'll see."

# *Chapter Seven*

She was dead.

There was no other explanation. She couldn't move, and she felt as if she was dying. She had to be dead.

"Rise and shine. Breakfast!"

Susan only groaned in response, until the door opened and Angela came bouncing in. "How are you feeling today?"

Susan buried her face in her pillow and muttered.

"What?" Angela said, coming closer.

Susan moaned.

"Uh-oh," Angela said before turning and bounding toward the door. "Uncle Jul! Better come quick. Dr. Susan is ill."

"No! Ang—" But Susan knew she was too late. She could hear the girl pounding down the hall, announcing her condition to the entire household.

Susan groaned and covered her head with the pillow.

Booted feet sounded on the floor, along with other sounds and voices. "Freckles?"

"Dr. Susan, I brought Uncle Jul...."

"Susan, what's the matter?" Laura said.

"What do you think is the matter? That fool brother of mine rode her into the ground yesterday," came Zach's voice from beside the bed.

Susan felt for and found the sheet before pulling it up over her head.

"Okay, okay. Let me have a look at her. Everyone leave, please. Except Laura. You want to stay as chaperone?" Julian said.

"Of course I will," she said so graciously that it put Susan immediately at ease. One thing they had been taught in medical school: never ever examine anyone without a chaperone.

She heard booted feet and murmurs before finally a door closed.

"Freckles? How are you feeling today?"

"How do you think I feel, Hawk? My back end is on fire. From my lumbar down." She thought a moment. "And up. Even my shoulders are hurting."

"Well, let's have a feel, then."

The covers went flying.

"Hey! I'm a doctor."

"And you're my patient. Come on, Freckles, cool it. I'd let you do the same thing if I were in your boots...er, pink shorts, that is."

Susan groaned with embarrassment. "So what? I wear pink. Some redheads can do that."

"You're not one of them, dear," he said, laughter in his voice.

"Stop that, Jul," Laura admonished. "Give the doctor some dignity."

Julian only chuckled as he examined her.

"Yes. There...and there and—ouch—there."

"Laura, do we have that liniment old Red made up for the horses?"

"For the *horses!*" Susan cried out, aghast.

"Hey, it works wonders on horses and humans alike."

"I keep some in my room for when Zach is in pain," Laura replied.

"Don't you ignore me, Hawk," Susan said, and flipped over. She immediately regretted it as her eyes crossed.

"No quick movements, Freckles," Julian

warned. "Will you get it and work it into her sore muscles, Laura? Then she can come downstairs for breakfast."

"Sure. You stay right there, Susan. Let me go get it and I'll be right back."

Laura hurried from the room, in her deputy's outfit.

"I'm really sorry about this, Freckles. Next time we'll take it slower. If it's any consolation, you caught on faster than anyone I've ever seen. That's one of the reasons I forgot you hadn't ridden before. You did great. You sure you haven't ridden before?"

"Where does a kid from New York ride?"

"From—"

"I'm back."

Julian turned to Laura. Susan saw the jar of stuff that looked like pig fat to her. No, she would not ask. With her luck that would be exactly what it was. Hokey potions. And up until now she'd thought Julian such a good doctor. "I'll leave her in your hands, Laura. We'll meet you downstairs for breakfast."

"Sure thing, Jul. Go. Mitch is here and wanted to talk to you."

Julian turned and hesitated at the doorway.

"Give it a day or two, Freckles, and you'll feel fine."

She didn't believe him, but she wasn't going to argue. Arguing would keep him there, and she only wanted whatever they thought might help relieve the pain.

When the door closed, Laura turned to Susan. "Want a bullwhip to take after that insensitive man?"

Susan rolled slowly back onto her stomach. "Give me two."

Laura laughed. Sitting down, she opened the jar. A rank smell drifted out. "Oh, groan, tell me I'm not smelling the treatment."

"I'm afraid so. But it does work wonders."

Cool ointment and gentle but sturdy hands touched her thigh and started working the ointment into her leg.

"How long have you worked as a deputy sheriff, Laura?" Susan said to take her mind off the fact that she was lying facedown on the bed while Hawk's sister-in-law rubbed pig fat into her legs. Okay, maybe not pig fat, maybe it was cow fat or chicken fat or…no, she wasn't going to think about it.

"Not quite a year."

"Really?"

"Yeah. I came out here about a year ago looking for my brother. That's when I met Zach and we eventually fell in love and married. I resigned from the force back in Louisiana and took Mitch up on a job offer here."

"You were a big-city cop?" Susan asked, surprised.

"You could say that."

"You fit in so well out here, though," Susan said.

Her muscles were slowly relaxing, and Susan was grateful for the work Laura was doing.

"I was ready for a change. I was chasing my father's dream instead of my own. I finally gave it up, and I love what I'm doing now."

"This is certainly different from where I grew up. There was always noise and people—everywhere."

"Do you miss all the people?" Laura asked as she worked on the next leg.

"My family mostly. But not where we live. It's not the safest neighborhood in the city. I hope to get them out of there one day."

"I was like that, too. Always watching out for my little brother." Laura continued to knead Susan's sore muscles. "God had to knock me flat on my back to teach me to let go and let Him be in control.''

Susan thought about that. ''I have trouble with that, too, I suppose,'' she finally said.

''Ah, well, that's the nice thing about God's grace. We're never too old to learn.''

''I wonder about that sometimes,'' Susan said.

''Oh, honey,'' Laura said, pausing. ''You aren't doubting God's grace, are you?''

Susan shook her head. ''Sometimes I do wonder if He really takes such a personal interest in our lives as I used to think He did.''

Laura rearranged Susan's sleep set and then sat back. ''Believe me, Susan, He does. He cares deeply. He sent His son. How much more can He care than that?''

Susan felt tears prick her eyes. ''Yeah. I guess over the past years it's been hard, being so far from home and everyone I know. It's just really been a trial. I had hoped, when school was over, to go back home to my family, but I'm out here now.''

She rolled over. Laura stood and pushed the covers back, helped her out of bed. ''Well, you have an adopted family right here, Susan. You'll always be welcome here, with us.''

Susan felt such a weight lift off her shoulders

that tears actually fell. She reached out and accepted the hug Laura offered. "Thank you. I think it's beautiful out here, but I am used to people, and yet through college and up until now I haven't had time to get to know anyone. It's just like all at once I'm missing my family an awful lot."

"Did you go home and see them before coming here?"

Susan nodded. "Chrissy is a teenager and so grown now, and my brother, Chaseon, is ready to start college. And two other sisters are adorable. Ten and fifteen. Of course, we can't leave out Rachel, either, who's special." She smiled softly. "They're a handful for Mom. It was hard saying goodbye." Susan released her. "I'm still stiff and don't think I'll be able to stand up straight," she muttered.

Laura laughed. "Probably not. Just wait. You'll be able to get revenge on him soon. I'll let you dress." Laura started toward the door, then paused, her hand on the knob, "And Susan, remember God is in control. Let Him guide you."

Susan nodded. She watched Laura leave and wished she could just learn to trust not having control and making her own destiny happen.

Laura marched down the hall and glowered at the men in the living room before passing on into the kitchen.

"Uh-oh, little brother, I'd say you're in trouble," Zach murmured to Julian.

"Me? What'd I do?" Julian asked, astonished at the glower Laura had turned on him.

"Could be you took the new doctor out riding and got her so sore she can't walk," Mitch murmured.

"I didn't mean to. She was riding so well I just forgot," Julian defended.

Zach shook his head and tsked. "Not something you should forget, especially with such a delicate-looking woman. I'll go see if I can calm Laura."

"Delicate, hmph," Julian said as Zach walked off.

"Yeah, delicate," Mitch said. "Be lucky Zach doesn't take you out back and explain the differences between a woman and a man again."

"I'm too old for that," Julian said, greatly offended.

"Well, yeah, I'd have figured that. But Susan is upstairs in bed because you forgot." Mitch shook his head. "Last time Zach did that I was seventeen. How old are you now, Jul?"

Julian threw his hands up in the air, disgusted. "I forgot. How many times do I have to tell you that?"

"I'm sure you did," Mitch said, grinning suddenly as he walked over and picked up a pillow from the sofa. Returning to the table, he paused by a chair and dropped the extra padding into a chair for Susan. "I'm just emphasizing it so maybe you'll think on it awhile."

Julian had opened his mouth to retort when the rest of the family came out of the kitchen carrying platters. At the same time Susan came down the hall and hobbled into the living room.

Julian watched his middle brother go and assist Susan into a chair. He scowled. Going over, Julian gave his brother a get-lost look, picked up Susan's napkin and dropped it into her lap. "There you go. How's the liniment helping?"

Susan smiled softly and nodded. "Thank you, Hawk."

Mitch chuckled.

Julian ignored him and moved around the table, taking his seat.

Zach bowed his head and prayed. Then they ate. As they ate, Julian watched how Zach and Mitch questioned Susan and pulled her into the family circle. Before long she was smiling, laughing and once again at ease. Actually, she was more at ease than he'd seen her before.

Laura especially made an effort to treat her more like a sister than a guest, and Angela took her cue from Laura and mimicked her. Julian did indeed have to ask himself why he had been so distant.

After all, she was his partner, for better or worse. No accidents had happened today and likely wouldn't. Perhaps if he worked with her, they'd develop a rapport and the patients wouldn't suffer—nor would he any longer.

As they finished their meal, Julian decided that was exactly what he'd do. He'd work on developing a rapport with her, a good working relationship, treat her like a partner and make sure she stayed healthy and happy for the patients'—and for his—benefit.

No time for anything more, he told himself. He'd just work on developing that professional relationship.

# Chapter Eight

Had he really thought to have a professional relationship with this woman? he wondered as he scraped the paint off his face and out of his hair.

"Quick! Get a wet towel. Just be still, Hawk. Try not to blink."

As if he was going anywhere. He couldn't see *to* go anywhere. Ugh, even his tongue tasted like paint. Of course, he'd had his mouth open when the paint holder had hit him square in the face. Man, he wasn't sure, but he thought his nose was broken. What had made Susan scramble backward like that? He'd tried to warn her there was a ladder there.

He heard feet scurrying back and then Freckles had him by the arm, leading him down the hall. "Ouch, ugh, be careful, Freckles, ugh—" *spit, spit* "—you're going to trip me." *Spit, spit.*

"Right in here."

He was pushed back and seated. A warm cloth hit his face.

"Ouch, my nose!" he exclaimed.

"Oh, this isn't going to work. Come here."

Susan grabbed him by the arm and started again down the hall, or a hall, with him in tow. When he felt the wind, he realized they were outside.

"Freckles. I need to—"

There was a sound of cranking and then she had him around the neck and cold—ice-cold— water from the outside hose hit him squarely in the face.

He sucked in a sharp breath and choked.

"Don't do that. Close your mouth."

He had no choice but to obey, or drown. He quickly did as told.

Water sprayed his face and hair. He scrunched his eyes closed despite the pain as Susan quickly ran her hand through his hair. At least she bent him at the waist to keep him from getting totally soaked.

Finally she dropped the hose and the tepid towel went around his hair. "Come on, let's get you inside before you freeze out here in this chilly weather."

"G-g-good idea," he chattered.

She dragged him toward the back door and inside. Looking at the cluttered hall, he wondered how he'd made it outside in one piece. Freckles guided him into a nearby room and sat him down on a chair. Turning to the worker at the door, she said, "Send someone for a fresh shirt from Dr. McCade's room."

She turned her attention back to Julian. "Now, Hawk, let me look at that nose and eye."

"Eye?"

Reaching up, he felt it, and sure enough his left eye was swelling. "I didn't notice because of the pain my nose is feeling. Of course, it's numb right now from cold."

"Oh, dear." Freckles clucked sympathetically before moving around him to pick up a light. "Lean your head back, Hawk, and let me look up into your nose—yes, just like that," she said, pushing his head back.

Gazing at the ceiling, he blinked, then blinked again. No...it wasn't...was it? Baby ducks, chicks, dinosaurs, birds all stared at him from the ceiling. "You have me in the pediatric room?"

"It's one of the few that's completely renovated," she said calmly.

"Don't try to placate me. Ouch!"

While he held his nose, she laid the instrument aside. Amazingly, when she lifted her hands to feel his nose, she said in a gentle voice, so caring and kind that it had him blinking to make sure this was the same Freckles Learner, "I know it hurts. And would I try to placate you?"

He should have known she was simply preparing for the kill. "Yes, you—ouch—would—ouch—stop poking!" His nose felt as if it was being bent out of joint.

"Stop fussing, Hawk, and let me examine you. I'm your doctor this time." Motherly voice. Why did he feel as if he belonged in the pediatric room all of the sudden?

Hawk groaned.

Susan grinned. "Do you realize you're our, well, *my,* first official patient at this clinic?"

Now, why hadn't Julian foreseen that? He should have. After all, every time he and Freckles were in the same room, disaster struck.

He'd probably end up being their most frequent patient, too.

"I don't think your nose is broken. You're going to have a shiner, though, for the next few days. And it's not going to be gone by Thursday. All of the Thanksgiving family pictures are going to show you with a black eye."

"Great. And my nose?"

"Well, the swelling should be down by then. Actually, it's not as bad as it seems. It's just really tender."

"You don't have to tell me that," Julian muttered. Exasperated, he asked, "Just why did you back away from me, Freckles, when I started toward you? I only wanted to check the spot in your eye."

Susan moved across the room and cleaned up the instrument she'd just used on Julian. He ignored that and waited for her to answer. Instead of a straight answer—why had he expected that from her?—she *complained* at him. "It was my turn to treat you. You'd already treated me once and I wasn't going to let you treat me twice in a row."

"Huh?" Julian gaped, confused.

Susan turned and smiled. "That's right. I had already looked at my eye, and it was a simple blood vessel broken. Though how I'm going to explain this one to Laura, I don't know.''

"Laura. What does she have to do with this?''

"She saw the bruises on my arm that morning, Hawk. And now this eye. She thinks you hit me.''

"She what?'' Hawk jumped off the table in shock.

"Well, who else do I know that might do such dastardly things?'' she asked innocently.

"I wouldn't do such dastardly things, Freckles, and you know that!''

"You made me ride until I couldn't walk,'' she muttered.

Julian stared, then scowled. "Oh, I see, this is payback for what I did. You're thoroughly enjoying treating me, aren't you? Either that or... Man, you're doing exactly what Zach does when he doesn't want to answer one of my questions. You changed the subject!''

Julian growled, planning not to let her get away with it. He had to take that from Zach, but not her. "So back to the original question. Why did you back up—''

"Manuel! Lita! You made it!'' Susan hurried over to the door, took the shirt from Manuel and tossed it at Julian. "Here you go, Hawk. We'll meet you in the lobby."

Julian knew what he'd seen in her eyes. Other than the injury. But he just couldn't be sure. Had she been looking at him as if she was interested in more than a professional relationship, or was he simply having delusions from Zach's words? Zach was going to drive him crazy. Julian dropped his head back, looking up at the ceiling and groaned. That woman was going to be the death of him.

"Señor McCade? He is going to be okay, yes?" Lita asked, her round little face creased with worry.

"Yes, yes, *sí*, Lita. He'll be just fine. He only had a minor accident. I'm so glad you could make it out today. Have you seen your room yet? Manuel, will you be staying here, too?"

"No, *señorita*. I have a family. I will go home at night to them. My wife is pregnant, *grande*." He motioned with his hands and grinned. Susan smiled at the small man.

"And you're certainly proud. Who is her doctor?"

Manuel shook his head. "She has no *doctora, señorita*. We have three babies already. No need for a doctor."

"That's not true, Manuel. You should have your wife come in. I tell you what. Since you are working here, we'll consider it part of your insurance, your job. Medical care comes with it."

Manuel shook his head. "No, *señorita*. I cannot. Dr. McCade. He won't like it."

"I won't like what?" Julian asked, coming out, tucking in his shirt.

"Manuel's wife is expecting a baby and pretty far along from what I understand. I was simply explaining to him that medical care was included for him and Lita while they worked here. I don't think he understood."

Julian nodded. Turning, he started a rapid-fire conversation in Spanish with Manuel, talking back and forth. Finally Manuel nodded. *"Muy bien. Sí, sí. Gracias, mi amigo."*

Julian turned back to Susan. "He understands now."

"I had no idea you spoke Spanish."

Julian grinned. "My dad's side of the family was from Spain. They settled here in America a long, long time ago. I have Mexican relatives, as well. Did you wonder why my skin isn't quite as pale as yours?"

Susan stared, then chuckled. "No. It never

crossed my mind. I mean, you're from Texas and lived on a ranch. I just figured you had a tan. So, you're fluent in Spanish.''

Julian chuckled. ''Well, it's very little anymore, but we still speak the language. A lot of people out here are bilingual. Since I was planning to be a doctor, I kept up my Spanish and worked hard to stay bilingual.''

Susan grinned. She turned to Lita. ''I guess I have to learn Spanish, don't I?''

She chuckled and rattled something off to Julian.

''What?'' Susan asked.

''Lita said she thinks I'll do just fine teaching you everything you need to know.''

Susan groaned. ''What a sexist remark,'' she said softly.

Lita just chuckled.

''Okay, okay. Let me show you where you'll sleep, Lita. Manuel, did you bring her suitcases? We've put you, Lita, downstairs near the back. The sleeping rooms are made up. I wasn't sure what you'd like so I had them paint it a pale peach. I hope that's okay.''

''*Sí, señorita.* It will be just fine for me.''

''I'm glad. After we get that done, I'd like to

talk over the filing system with you. We can see about getting something set up.''

"In Spanish or English, *señorita?*''

Susan paused. ''Ah, well, there is a question, isn't it?''

She led Lita off down the hall to her room, leaving both men in the lobby to handle baggage. ''We got the forms in today. They're in English. I suppose we'll do the filing in English and if the forms are in Spanish, well...''

"It is okay, *señorita.* I speak English well and write it, too. Mostly.''

Relieved, Susan nodded. ''I'll learn, I suppose, since I'll be here two years.''

Lita moved into the room and muttered something in Spanish, obviously good if the joy on her face was any indication, then she nodded. ''*Sí*, we need doctors bad. Good doctors who will stay. People do not trust new doctors, but they will trust little Julian. Most know him from when he ran the range.''

"Well, I hope they come to trust me, too.''

"They will, *señorita.* They see how he makes the eyes at you, and they will know what I know. He is soon to be your *esposo.* They will accept you then.''

*Espresso?* Susan shook her head, not understanding what coffee had to do with the conversation. Must mean something else. She vowed to learn the language soon. "Well, he makes the eyes at me because he doesn't trust me, Lita. But he will soon. When he figures out I am not quite this klutzy all the time."

Lita chuckled and said something else in Spanish, then snapped out instructions to Manuel, who was just coming into the room, with Julian behind him.

Susan backed up. "When you finish here, we'll be around, Lita. Thank you."

Lita nodded and waved her off, still talking to Manuel in that rapid-fire language that she didn't understand.

Susan turned and hurried out. Julian followed at a slower pace. "Don't worry, Freckles, you'll learn."

"Yeah. It's just so foreign. I have heard people around talking in Spanish, but I didn't know until today just how prevalent the language is here. When she asked me which language to put the forms in—"

"Yeah. Try not to worry. It'll be fine."

Susan nodded. "Well, what do you think?" she asked, walking down the hall and pointing.

"I don't recall ordering wallpaper."

Susan grinned. "You didn't. But the tiny cacti with budding flowers go well with the rust, brown and white colors. And it cuts down the dark and makes the rooms look bigger and brighter, which is important when you're dealing with sick people."

Julian nodded. "Does this take us over our budget?"

Susan shook her head. "Actually, it went under the budget by just over a hundred dollars."

"But wallpaper runs more than paint."

"I struck a deal. They donated it at cost with the agreement that if they were in an accident of some sort, their blood would be free."

Julian blinked.

"Come on, Hawk. That's not a whole lot off the price. We can surely pick that up."

"Actually, I was thinking that was ingenious."

Susan grinned. "Glad you think so. Then you won't be upset when you hear what I did about the furniture you ordered."

Julian frowned. "Just what did you do?"

"You had new furniture in there. I called them up and told them the prices were just too much and canceled it. When they panicked at losing such a good sale, I suggested that we'd keep the furniture at a reduced price and allow them to furnish our waiting room in return for putting up advertisements for their store in each room. They're small, cute little plaques that say Donated By and then the store's name.''

"So, you didn't get rid of the furniture?" he asked, relieved.

"Well, just the bedroom furniture. They wouldn't give me the deal I wanted, so I found some used furniture at different stores. It's almost as good, and no one will see it except staff."

"I had no idea you knew how to haggle."

Susan chuckled. "I'm very good at haggling. With four younger sisters and a brother I learned really early how to get the best deal for each dollar spent."

There she went again, Julian thought. Just when he thought he had the woman figured out, she threw in a curveball. What use would she have to haggle? Had her family had hardships or—

Distracted by her gentle laugh, he let the question slide and listened as she went into a story about one of her siblings, though he didn't hear a lot.

Watching the glow on her face, he realized

that being around Freckles Learner wasn't as awful as he had once thought. Dangerous, yes. Awful...

Only time would tell.

# Chapter Nine

"We're open."

Julian's chuckle drew Susan's gaze. "You find that funny?"

"It was the way you said it, or perhaps that this is the sixth time you've said it."

Susan paced to the window, then dropped into a nearby chair. She was dressed in tan slacks and a white blouse today. She wore a lab coat, the pockets full of little goodies she needed to perform her job.

Julian, on the other hand, wore a faded pair of jeans with a dark blue button-down shirt and his tennis shoes that looked older than he did. He seemed totally at ease. She dragged the toe of her shoe across the marbled tiles in disgust.

"No patients. I'm just wondering if they realize we are open."

"Word will get around."

"*Sí, señorita*. My Manuel and I, we tell the people. But it will take time."

Susan smiled at Lita. "I suppose so."

"What did you expect, Freckles?" Julian asked conversationally.

"I'm not sure. Patients lined up outside. You know, like at most free clinics? The lines go outside sometimes as people wait for free medical treatment. Or even reduced-fee treatment."

"Maybe eventually, Freckles. But I think we're going to have to give it time."

Going over, he dropped down next to her. "You weren't in church with us yesterday."

The low tones sent shivers down her back. "I just—I don't fit in there, Hawk. I don't talk like the people here, act like them. Some of them are already avoiding me...."

Julian reached out and picked up her hand, squeezing it gently. "We missed you. As for those who don't think you belong? You're a doctor. We need doctors here right now. And I don't think anyone is going to object to your being in church."

"What are you doing?" Susan's pulse had

skyrocketed the minute he picked up her hand. But to feel the rough texture of his darker callused finger running over the lighter, softer skin on the back of her hand—it seemed so, so intimate.

Julian looked down and suddenly dropped her hand. "Is that a scar? I was just examining—"

"Doctor Juliano. I come for treatment."

Both of their gazes turned to the door. There stood a young man, dark hair hanging shaggily over his ears, his thin face grinning from ear to ear at Hawk while he held an arm wrapped in some sort of white cloth. At least the overalls he wore were clean. His hands weren't. And that white cloth was dingy. Worried, Susan stood.

Julian strode across the room. Of course he would. She was still gathering her wits about her. What timing. She had liked the feel of Julian's hand on hers and had thought to...to what?

Shaking her head, she followed Julian and the boy down the hall.

She didn't understand much, as they both spoke Spanish. However, she did understand *yuck* and could think of no better way to exclaim at what she saw when he held his hand out.

"What in west Texas is that on your wound?"

The bandage covered with dirt wasn't what she professed shock over. Nor was it the dirt under his nails and caked around his knuckles. It was the brown goo packed into a one-inch wound.

Julian poured some betadine into a bowl and eased the boy's hand down into it. "Meet José, Susan."

José grinned at her, one of his front teeth missing. "It's a poultice to keep the bad out of the injury."

"A poultice?"

Susan knew what that was, but hadn't heard of those being used in ages. Evidently, though, José didn't think she understood. He began rattling off the ingredients. When he got to cow paddies, to put it nicely, she stopped him.

"I've heard enough." Indeed. Out of everything she had seen in medical school, nothing had prepared her for this.

"Want to make yourself useful, Freckles, or are you going to stand there gawking?" Julian said in a low voice as he slipped on rubber gloves and started scrubbing the young boy's hand. José was rattling off something in Spanish that elicited a nod and grunt from Julian at the appropriate times.

Turning, she went across the room. "Is this

poultice a normal practice here?'' she couldn't help but ask as she pulled out the chromatic sutures and a suture tray to set up for sewing.

''By some. When it's bleeding heavily, they only know to stop the bleeding. Some use different homemade healing poultices. Others find different ways. The education level here medically is very low. One thing I'd like to see this clinic implement eventually is first aid classes for the people out this way.''

''I'd be glad to see that,'' Susan murmured. Moving the tray over by him, she set everything out and then stepped back.

Julian moved gracefully as he worked on the patient. Susan marveled at how he kept the young boy entertained while he deadened the area, how at ease he was as, bit by bit, he stitched up the wound.

She offered her help, but Julian refused and cut the threads himself. Susan knew he still didn't trust her. And that was okay, for now. She'd teach him, though. He'd learn that he could trust her.

''*Señorita?*''

Susan turned and hurried over to where Lita stood near the door. ''Yes?''

''*Señor* McCade is here.''

Glancing back to where Julian still worked, Susan decided he wouldn't miss her—which was saddening in a way. But it was better than standing there feeling helpless. Going out with Lita, she walked into the lobby and found Zach McCade waiting.

He smiled and nodded, hat in hand. "Ma'am. How's it going?"

Susan couldn't help but return the smile. Zach reminded her of herself in many ways. "Our first patient. Haw—Julian is stitching him up now. How can I help you?"

"Can you spare a minute to walk with me?"

Susan glanced to Lita. "I'll be outside."

"Of course," Lita said and sat down at her desk, going back to work.

Susan walked out the door by Zach's side. "So, what's up?"

Zach shook his head and chuckled. "Nothing. Jul's givin' you a hard time, is he?"

"Does it show?" she asked, flushing.

Zach smiled. "A bit. Of course, I'm an oldest child, too. I recognize that pained look of patience in your eyes."

Susan couldn't help it—she laughed. "I tend to be accident-prone whenever he is around, so

I can hardly blame him for his wariness, now, can I?''

"That'll pass," Zach said. He sounded so confident Susan had to nod in agreement.

"Here we are."

Zach stopped by the broken-down stables and pointed inside.

Susan looked inside and gasped. "Oh, my. They're beautiful." Hurrying inside, she strode up to a beautiful bay in one stall and examined it. "Is this Redwood?"

Zach, who had followed, reached out and stroked the mare's neck. "She sure is. She'll fit your personality just fine. The other one there is Blackwell. He's for Julian."

Susan paused in petting the bay's nose. Glancing up at him sideways, she studied Zach. "Why aren't you telling Julian this?"

Zach grinned. "Laura sent these over. I'm afraid if I tell Jul, he might just want to shoot the messenger. He doesn't want help from his brothers right now."

Susan nodded, having noted that. She didn't understand it, thinking he had a wonderful family, but she definitely knew he didn't like it. Realization dawned. "You want me to tell him."

Zach leaned back against the post. "I think

he'll take it much better from you, yes. However, if you're worried he'll get upset, when he's done with the patient I'll stick around and tell him.''

Susan debated. Then she decided. "We do need horses if we have to go out where cars can't reach."

"Laura's thoughts exactly."

"And they will be a benefit to our business."

"Yep."

Susan grinned. "And I've wanted a horse."

Zach returned her grin. "Sold."

Susan actually giggled. "Thanks, Zach. Send Laura my love and tell her we thank her profusely."

"Profusely, huh? Julian, too?" His grin widened.

"Yes. Julian, too. At least, he will before the night is out." Susan winked. "I've handled a younger brother and sisters. He'll simply have to accept the gift and realize some things are just meant to be."

Zach hooted. "You tell him that and I'm not responsible for what he says." He headed toward the door and paused in the parking lot by his truck. "You tell Julian I said hi. Any chance you'll be coming for dinner tonight?"

Susan shook her head. "This is our first dinner in the clinic. Lita wants to fix something
special."

Zach nodded. "Don't be a stranger."

Susan waved and watched him leave.

She liked Zach. For that matter, she liked
Mitch, too. It was a shame that Julian got so
prickly any time they came out here to poke
around. It was only concern. But he saw it as
trying to control.

The teenage boy came out and mounted his
horse, calling a goodbye to her. She waved to
him then turned to Julian, who had come strolling out after him.

"Lita said Zach was here."

"You just missed him." Susan could still see
the dust trail kicking up from Zach's truck and
trailer as they traveled down the long narrow
road.

"I see that. Why didn't he wait? Did he say
what he wanted?"

Susan saw the curiosity as he stared after his
brother and decided now was as good a time as
any. "Yeah, he told me what he wanted. Come
here."

Susan hurried off, leaving Julian no choice but
to follow if he wanted to find out what his

brother had said. To say she was a bit nervous was an understatement. But then again, to say she wasn't excited about the prospect of showing Hawk the horses wasn't true, either.

"Freckles?"

"In here, Hawk." Susan hurried into the darkened barn, Julian right behind her.

Turning, she smiled at him through the dimness. "Will you stop looking like the roof is going to fall in on your head?" she muttered, exasperated. He didn't have to think her capable of *that*, did he?

"I didn't say that," Julian defended, and she could tell by his voice it was what he thought. "Where'd the horses come from?"

Uh-oh. He'd finally seen them. "Aren't they beautiful?" Susan turned and hurried over to the first one. "This is Redwood and that one is Blackberry." She tried to remember if that was the right name or not.

"You didn't answer me, Freckles. Where'd the horses come from?" His voice vibrated with suppressed anger.

Susan turned. "Where do you think they came from, Hawk?" She couldn't help the chiding in her voice. He just reminded her so much of a naughty child right now.

Anger blazed across his features. "Zach can just come back and get the horses. You won't have them."

He turned and started toward the door and Susan snapped. She'd had it with this thing between him and his family. "No. You won't. I'm keeping them."

Julian's face was priceless when he turned to look at her. She'd never seen that look before.

"Close your mouth or you'll catch flies," she goaded.

"I said—" His gaping mouth snapped shut.

"I don't care, Julian. This ongoing battle between you and your brother can stay between you two. Laura wanted us to have the horses. If you don't want Blackberry, then I'll keep them both. I never had a horse. I want a horse." She smiled patiently. "So now I have two horses. So if you'll excuse me?"

She walked past him and strode off toward the clinic.

Julian stood stupefied, staring after her. What had gotten into her? He'd never seen Freckles angry before. Freckles. That didn't fit her right now. As he watched her storm across the yard, he realized she had hidden facets of her personality he'd never seen.

A small smile curved his lips. "Freckles angry. Who would have ever thought?"

Slowly he left the barn and started back to the clinic, anticipating just what other facets might be revealed in the coming weeks.

# *Chapter Ten*

The sound of clucking was his first clue today wasn't going to be any different from any other day since he'd met Freckles Learner.

Julian lay still, certain he hadn't just heard a cluck and muffled shout near his window.

Flapping wings, a scuttle and a low, growling "baa..caw" made him open his eyes to the pre-dawn light.

The distant sound of the clinic door opening, then voices, let him know the others were all up.

Squinting, he was looking about his small room trying to identify what sounded strangely like a fowl when the feathered beast landed right on his chest.

# HOW TO VALIDATE YOUR
# EDITOR'S FREE GIFT!
# "THANK YOU"

1 Peel off the FREE GIFTS SEAL from front cover. Place it in the space provided at right. This automatically entitles you to receive two free books and an exciting mystery gift.

2 Send back this card and you'll get 2 Love Inspired® novels. These books have a combined cover price of $9.00 in the U.S. and $10.50 in Canada, but they are yours to keep absolutely FREE!

3 There's no catch. You're under no obligation to buy anything. We charge nothing—ZERO—for your first shipment. And you don't have to make any minimum number of purchases—not even one!

4 We call this line Love Inspired because each month you'll receive novels that are filled with joy, faith and true Christian values. The stories will lift your spirits and gladden your heart! You'll like the convenience of getting them delivered to your home well before they are in stores. And you'll like our discount prices too!

5 We hope that after receiving your free books you'll want to remain a subscriber. But the choice is yours—to continue or cancel, anytime at all! So why not take us up on our invitation, with no risk of any kind. You'll be glad you did!

6 Don't forget to detach your FREE BOOKMARK. And remember... just for validating your Editor's Free Gift Offer, we'll send you 2 novels and a gift, *ABSOLUTELY FREE!*

## *YOURS FREE!*

*We'll send you a fabulous mystery gift absolutely FREE, simply for accepting our no-risk offer!*

## The Editor's "Thank You" Free Gifts Include:

- Two Christian romance novels
- An exciting mystery gift

PLACE
FREE GIFTS
SEAL
HERE

# YES! I have placed my Editor's "thank you" Free Gifts seal in the space provided above. Please send me the 2 FREE books and gift for which I qualify. I understand that I am under no obligation to purchase anything further, as explained on the opposite page.

**303 IDL CQEM**

**103 IDL CQEN**
**(LI-EC-01/00)**

| | | | | | | | | | | | | | | | | | |
|---|---|---|---|---|---|---|---|---|---|---|---|---|---|---|---|---|---|

NAME                  (PLEASE PRINT CLEARLY)

| | | | | | | | | | | | | | | | | | |
|---|---|---|---|---|---|---|---|---|---|---|---|---|---|---|---|---|---|

ADDRESS

APT.#          CITY

STATE/PROV.          ZIP/POSTAL CODE

## Thank You!

BUSINESS REPLY MAIL
FIRST-CLASS MAIL    PERMIT NO. 717    BUFFALO, NY

POSTAGE WILL BE PAID BY ADDRESSEE

STEEPLE HILL READER SERVICE
3010 WALDEN AVE
PO BOX 1867
BUFFALO NY 14240-9952

NO POSTAGE
NECESSARY
IF MAILED
IN THE
UNITED STATES

"Aagh!" Julian jerked, shocked, as he came face-to-beak with a white-feathered, red-jowled chicken of the female persuasion.

Beady little eyes stared right at him, and its head was bobbing.

"What in the—"

*Crash.*

Julian's door flew open.

Freckles, her hair sticking up in every direction, came running in, broom in hand. Manuel and Lita and a young girl of maybe ten years all headed right toward him.

The chicken obviously realized danger when she saw it. Her claws dug into him, wings flapped and she let out a sound that would have wakened the dead and nearly deafened him.

"Freckles?" Julian grabbed at the chicken, trying to move it. "Freckles! No!"

Julian dived under the covers as the bristle end of the broom came swinging his direction.

*Thud.* Right in the chest.

"Get off him!"

*Smack.* The abdomen.

"Shoo!"

*Oh, no,* Julian thought with horror as he felt the flapping chicken move down his body.

*Bang.* Relieved it was only his thighs she hit, he shoved the cover off his head.

"Get on out of here!" Freckles said this with a look of worry on her face as she pushed with the broom at the bird.

"Freckles!" Despite the worry and frustration on her face, Julian didn't like that little spark of determination he spotted in her eye.

"I'm sorry, Hawk. I've never been around fowl before. It won't listen!"

She proceeded to chase the poor helpless bird around the room.

Julian saw her backing it into a corner and leapt from the bed, grabbing her from behind just in time. "Enough!" he shouted.

*"Alto,"* he repeated to the others in the room.

Susan fell back against him, and he could feel her heavy breathing, smell hay in her hair and a soft sweet scent that he had never noticed before. Nor had he noticed how small she was or how vulnerable she felt in his arms. He stared at the curve of her jaw, then allowed his gaze to drop to where his arms surrounded her, his hands holding her hands.

The pitiful squawk of the outraged hen brought his head up.

"It scared the horses," Freckles informed him.

"Was this before or after you had the broom?"

"I was only trying to run it back into the lobby where we decided to keep it."

"Keep it?" Dread grew in the pit of his stomach. "What do you mean, keep it?"

"*Señor.* It is from my mom for my brother you treated. We pay you with a good hen."

Julian reluctantly released Freckles and turned to the young girl. "*Gracias, mi chiquita,*" he said gently, smiling at her. Glancing to Lita, he waited for an explanation.

Lita quickly explained as Manuel went forward and gathered the chicken into his arms. "It is a pet they had. One they did not kill for food. She lay eggs for them. They offer her as payment for what you did for José yesterday. They say his hand is much better. The chicken's name is Hester."

Lita turned to the little girl and thanked her.

Julian turned back to Freckles, who still held the broom in front of her. "Sometimes people pay by barter here. It's a way of retaining their pride while accepting help. So, it looks like we have a chicken," he said gently to her before carefully reaching out to take the broom. A lethal weapon in her hands he did not want at this moment. She still eyed the chicken warily as Manuel strolled casually out of the room.

She relinquished her weapon. Then she turned to him. "I'm sorry, Julian. It just wouldn't listen."

"So you chased it with a broom?"

Freckles frowned. "I was trying to get it off the chair. I thought its claws might tear the cloth."

She appeared so helpless as she gazed up at him in mute appeal. "City thugs I might be able to face, but not a chicken. I guess I've got a bit more to learn."

Aw, poor thing, Julian found himself thinking. Reaching out, he grabbed her by her shoulders and pulled her into his arms. Giving her a tight hug, he said, "You're doing fine. Country life just takes a bit of getting used to. And as we're going to be doctors out here for the next two year—"

Her gasp cut him off. Releasing her, he asked, "What is it, Freckles?"

"I forgot I need your help. In the lobby. Now. We have patients."

He watched Freckles turn and rush out of the

room. Patients? Plural. Wondering what could get Freckles so distracted—well, okay, he thought, she got distracted easily—he dressed and headed toward the lobby. He hadn't heard voices. No one had wakened him. Yet Freckles had changed in an instant from frustrated city girl to what he would describe as all professional-minded businesswoman.

He wasn't sure what he expected to find when he entered the lobby, but it wasn't a room packed full of people. His stunned gaze traveled over the people there.

Some he knew from when he was a kid, and they called out greetings. Others he didn't know. All were there for various reasons. Looking over at Lita, he said, "Organize these into the most serious first, can you, Lita?"

"*Sí*, Doctor."

Julian immediately set to work treating patients.

It was two hours later before he got his first break and went to his office to work up the reports for the hospital.

As the door opened Freckles looked up, frazzled, exhausted, but strangely exhilarated. "Last patient?"

Julian nodded. "For now. I'm sure everyone

who can go is at work. And those too sick to attend work probably didn't make it in."

A sound behind Julian drew her gaze and she gaped. "Don't look now, but you have company."

Julian grimaced. "Again?"

A small chuckle escaped Susan's throat. "So, the rumors are true."

She watched him cross to his desk and sit down. The *tap tap tap* of tiny claws followed him.

"I don't know, Freckles. What are the rumors?" Julian asked mildly as he pulled out papers to fill out for the hospital.

Susan rolled her pen between her fingers, grinning. "That Hester has taken a liking to you and is following you all over the clinic."

Hester the chicken chose that moment to flap her wings and cluck.

Julian winced.

Susan laughed.

"It's not funny," he muttered, and Susan took pity on him.

"Maybe not, but do you know, that stupid chicken following you around put the kids at ease? I can't tell you how many laughed and giggled and didn't fight me on immunizations as they chattered away about the chicken following you around.''

''Well, if you find it so amusing, why don't we let it follow you?''

Susan dropped her pen and stretched, laughing gaily. ''I don't think so, Hawk.'' Her laughter died, and she soberly studied the man she cared about. He was one of the few people she had ever felt she could trust, could talk to, could simply be around without pressures. Now, if she could turn off her feelings of attraction so easily she might not end up killing him in the process of their working relationship. Her mind just went south, though, when he was in the same room. But now, with what she wanted to ask, she didn't lose her train of thought or get lost in those deep brown eyes or his wide shoulders. No, this was something that had really disturbed her today. ''I do want to discuss a problem with you, though.''

''Oh?'' Hawk paused in shuffling the pile of folders on his desk to look up at Susan in query.

Susan paused when Lita bustled in, firing off a scolding at Hester—in Spanish, of course—before scooping up the fowl with great apologies. ''I am going with Manuel for lunch. I will be back when you open back up, *señor, seño-rita.*''

"Okay, Lita," Hawk said, and she bustled out. "Now." Hawk turned to Susan. "You said there was a problem?"

"Yes." Susan hesitated, looking at Hawk. He was so strong, so sure, so steady out here in his hometown. She, on the other hand, felt lost, alone and at the moment confused. "Why does it seem the people here don't trust me as they trust you?"

Hawk considered the question—she had to give him that much. "Have you had any more accidents today I don't know about?"

His question hurt. Susan wouldn't tell him that, because she couldn't blame him for asking. It was only when she was around him she was a disaster waiting to happen. But Hawk didn't see that. Maybe one day he would, but not now. So, instead of getting angry, she simply shook her head. "No. But a large percentage of them asked when they could see you, even as I was treating them."

"It might be, Freckles," he said, a hint of apology reflecting in his eyes. "A lot of the people here are, well, different than what you might find in a more developed area of the country. If

I had my guess, I'd say many just can't see you as a doctor.''

Susan flushed, but not with embarrassment. Anger curled her toes as she digested his words. ''You're kidding.''

He shook his head. ''I'm sorry, Freckles. I'm not certain, but I'd guess that is part of the problem. The other part is that they know me, and I speak their language. Please, don't be too upset. In time they'll stop seeing you as a woman and see you as a doctor.''

Susan wanted to say, *Like you*, but then that wasn't true, either. ''When will *you* start seeing me as a doctor, Julian?''

She could tell she had caught him off guard by the way his eyes widened and his mouth hung open.

''I know you're a doctor,'' he finally said.

Susan shook her head. ''No, in your eyes I'm simply a—''

A loud crash of shattering glass sounded from the front of the clinic. Susan gasped and jumped up. ''What was that?''

Hawk stood, too, and started around his desk. ''I'm not sure.''

Susan rushed out of the room.

''Wait, Susan!'' Hawk called, but Susan

didn't. She just knew someone had entered the clinic and was injured or had fallen. Flying down the hall, she burst into the lobby and saw half a dozen masked men in the process of what looked like lifting the sofa through the window.

They froze at her entrance.

All of them except the one she hadn't seen, that is.

"Well, it seems we meet again."

Strong, muscled arms slipped around her waist from behind and pulled her back against a rock-hard body. The smell of musky aftershave tickled her nose, and the rough feel of a stubbled jaw scratched the tender skin of her cheek.

That was all she noted before she was jerked around to face the hall. Susan gasped in pain as her ribs felt pressed to meet her backbone at the action.

"Now, now, Julian, just slow down there."

"What do you want, Noble?" Julian demanded, slowing to a stop in the hallway, his face a mask of frustration and a hint of—unease, anger, fear? Susan had never seen the emotions she saw in his eyes right now, and she wasn't sure how to read them.

Then the name registered. Susan stiffened, realizing the man from the café who had given her such a hard time the other day was the very man who held her captive in his steely grip right now.

"You know my name, do you, little lady?" the awful man crooned before laughing low, sending a tingle of fear down her spine. "You should have taken me up on that offer of a date."

"Let her go."

Julian's deep voice vibrated with anger, surprising Susan and evidently Noble, too, for the arm gripped so tightly about her waist eased momentarily. She sucked in a breath, prepared to jerk away, but the arm tightened back around her.

"Don't you be trying anything, now. You either, Juls," Noble crooned in a syrupy sweet voice. "I'm only trying to protect you from these masked men," he said, and pointed over his shoulder. Susan knew he was speaking of the men trashing the place—his men, she was certain. "So many just think this clinic is going to drag all the riffraff into town. No reason to provide so much free stuff for loafers," he muttered. "Yes, sirree, this sure isn't a good idea. I guess these men must be some of the ones who don't agree with you and your plans."

Julian snorted. "Get real, Noble. Those are your men, and I'm going to..."

"You're going to what?"

His arm tightened around Susan, drawing a wince from her. One hand moved up to caress her neck. Susan felt herself pale. She could smell the alcohol on his breath. She knew drunks could be very unpredictable. Silently she started praying.

"Call your brother to come protect you? Poor Julian never did get a chance to be his own man with two older brothers."

A loud crash from behind them made Susan jump. Noble leaned down and whispered against her ear, "There now, little lady, don't let that scare you none." Then he kissed her neck.

"Enough," Julian said in a low voice, and started forward.

Susan shuddered in utter revulsion. Then she did what any normal modern woman would do. Dropping her hands from where they'd clutched at Noble's arm, she hurled back her forearm in a forceful blow to his groin.

Noble let out an unearthly howl, sounding more like a wounded animal than human. He dropped to his knees.

Susan gasped, giddy with relief, knees knocking with fear and strangely paralyzed as she watched her attacker lie there moaning. She was a doctor. She had hurt him. Then she heard the shouts of the masked men. Her gaze rose to them.

Pure hatred glared back at her from one man's eyes.

Julian rushed forward. Grabbing her arm, he took off down the hall. She knew all of this had taken less than two seconds, but for her, time seemed to have slowed to a crawl that would make a turtle seem fast.

"Come on," he said, and continued dragging her down the hall.

"Hey!" one of the thugs yelled, and started after them.

Susan stumbled, gasping for breath as she tried to keep up with Julian. Glancing over her shoulder, she panicked. "They're right behind us!"

The man wearing the dark brown bandanna over his head and mouth reached for her, and brushed her blouse. *Please, Jesus. Help!* she silently cried as she stumbled forward toward Julian, dodging the hand, the cart, a ladder, a paint bucket.

God answered her plea, from a very unexpected source. At that very moment Hester took it into her heart to try to fly. Swooping down from the top of one of the many ladders in the hallway, she flapped her wings, squawking loudly, and flew for all she was worth. She made about two feet before landing right in the face of the man reaching for Susan.

The man screamed and backpedaled into the others. It reminded her of the domino effect. One by one they fell to the ground amid ladders, a cart—even one of the cans of paint went flying.

Julian didn't give her much time to watch, though, as he continued to pull her behind him. Reluctantly she turned her head and dodged the rest of the objects, following Julian as he rushed into their office.

Once inside he slammed the door, locked it and blocked it before grabbing for the cell phone.

Julian hit the buttons, but nothing happened. Looking down at the cell phone, he stared in disbelief. "It's run down. Someone left it on."

He looked directly at her.

Susan shook her head. "Oh, no, don't you blame that on me. *I* know how to use a cell phone."

"Well, I didn't do it!" Julian exclaimed, and

dropped the phone. Going to the window, he looked out.

"I am not going out that window," she said.

He frowned. "I don't think you'd fit."

Susan gasped. "I'm not *that* big, Julian McCade!"

Julian turned, bewilderment on his face. "I didn't say that."

"You said I wouldn't fit through the window!" Susan cried out, angry over the fact that her hips were a bit wider than deemed acceptable by today's standards and he'd had the nerve to comment on it.

"I just meant—"

"Oh, I know what you meant!" Going over, she grabbed a chair and dragged it to the window. "But I certainly can fit through there." Climbing onto the chair, she shoved the window up and slipped her hands to the edge. "And I'll pro-o-o—"

Strong hands grabbed her by her waist and hauled her back in.

Off balance she fell backward and they both kept going.

A loud "oooaf" sounded from under her. Susan's head conked something hard. Julian groaned. *Oh, no,* Susan thought dismally. *Here we go again.*

# *Chapter Eleven*

She lay there stunned, aware only of Hawk's arms wrapped tightly around her waist.

A short, gasping voice wheezed out into the strangely quiet room "I have...a cell phone...in my...back."

"Huh?" *Cell phone?* Susan, still dazed from the fall, vaguely realized what Julian had said. Then his words managed to merge and take on a form of coherence in her foggy brain. *Cell phone!* "Oh!"

Shocked, Susan realized she lay sprawled haphazardly on Julian, pinning him against the desk. She shifted to move off to the left, but Julian groaned. "Oh, dear," she whispered, and wiggled toward the right, feeling around, grabbing at the desk.

Julian moaned.

"Oh, oh no," she said, distressed. Shoving back with both hands, she tried to push herself straight off him to keep from causing him any more pain.

"You're... killing...me, Freckles!"

"You won't be still!" she cried out.

"I'm trying to *protect* myself!"

Suddenly warm, strong hands curved around her waist and rolled her to her right. She landed with a thud, face first on the desk.

Julian immediately stood and moved off across the room. Dropping his hands to his knees and gasping, he stared over at her balefully.

Susan pushed away from the desk and worked to straighten her hair. Then she straightened her blouse. Finally she smoothed her slacks.

"Expecting company?" he asked.

Her eyes widened. "Certainly not. I was only trying to show you I could go out that window."

"That's not what I meant about the window, Freckles." Slowly he straightened, looking like an old man. Every movement elicited a wince from her as he scowled and muttered before finally managing to stand straight. "I was checking to make sure it was locked so Noble and his men couldn't get in.''

Susan's eyes widened, then she blushed. ''Oh.'' Awkwardly, and a bit painfully, she scrambled back up into the chair and closed and locked the window. ''There.''

Julian managed a sigh along with a look of acceptance. ''I heard a truck pulling off when I was dragging you back inside. I think they're already gone.''

Susan nodded. Then sat down on what she thought was a chair. The floor made a perfect seat as far as she was concerned. Anything did at the moment. It was that or fall flat on her face.

''Whoa!'' Julian was across the room in two strides and pulling her up into his arms.

He felt so good. Muscles bunched, a firm chest was there to lean against. He smelled of antiseptic and latex gloves. And she had never smelled anything better in her life. Inching her arms around his neck, she dropped her head to his shoulder and shuddered. ''I just wanted to sit down.''

She wasn't going to admit that the pain of the ordeal had just hit her. He was a doctor. He knew that. But maybe, just maybe, he'd forgotten that from medical class. She could only hope.

Who was she kidding? Of course he hadn't. He was a wonderful doctor.

"Of course you did," he murmured softly.

Susan was in love. It hit her between the eyes. It wasn't attraction or an awkward desire, but love. When he could have taken the final blow to kill what was inside her, he ignored it and told her what she wanted to hear.

She wouldn't admit that the tears in her eyes were from that one act of gentleness. It was simply aftereffects. Yes, that was all it was. "The floor was fine," she whispered, knowing she sounded pitiful but unable to cope with the realization of just how much she loved this man on top of everything else.

"But I'd rather have you here."

Susan swallowed, certain she had heard him wrong.

He evidently thought he'd heard himself wrong, too, because he said so. "I didn't say what it sounded like. I mean, I am glad Noble didn't...that is...it's my turn to play doctor."

And just like that the tender moment was past. He shifted, picked her up, laid her on the couch and reached for her, running his hands over her arms, ribs, legs. "You hurting anywhere?"

She shifted and squirmed, trying to get away from his touch, embarrassed, since her entire world had just shifted within her heart. He wouldn't let her escape as he professionally inspected her.

"Bruised ribs, a bit shaken, but you look okay other than that."

"Thank you, Doctor," Susan said tartly.

Julian ignored the sharp tone in her voice, not even questioning why it was there. He only lifted an eyebrow in amusement and grinned. "You're welcome." He started across the room before adding softly, "Doctor."

She gaped.

He paused at the door. "You stay in here until I can make sure Noble is gone. If anything happens, do not open this door."

"God intervened!" Susan suddenly said.

Hawk glanced at her in question.

"Hester," Susan said, remembering the valiant actions of the hen earlier.

Slowly he nodded. "Yeah. I guess she's our guardian angel, huh, Freckles?"

Freckles smiled back, tenderness in her eyes. "Yeah, she is."

"I'll go look and be right back. Then we'll decide what to do next."

Susan shook her head and sat up, still a bit shaky. "You aren't going alone," she said.

Julian frowned. "Now, Susan. You can't tell me you really want to face those thugs if they're out there."

"You're right. I can't. I'll just have to believe God will go before us."

"Ayyyiee, aaayyyiee!"

"Lita!" the two said in unison.

Julian quickly unlocked the door and started down the hall, not waiting for Freckles. He heard her right behind him. Freckles had a mind of her own. He knew if he told her to go back, she'd ignore him, so the only thing he could do was make sure it was safe before she got there.

He'd nearly had heart failure earlier when he'd run into the room and seen the thugs and Noble, who was so drunk he hadn't been able to stand up straight. Noble had gripped Susan, nearly knocking her over at one point. His hands on her were totally unacceptable. Even worse had been the fear in Susan's eyes.

Julian hadn't known what to do. Everything in him had screamed to attack the guy who was hurting Susan. But that would have been insanity.

So instead he'd prayed for God to give Susan strength and him knowledge of how to handle the situation.

When Susan had struck Noble Julian had been impressed. He shuddered again, swearing never to make her angry with him, yet secretly proud of what she'd done.

Getting her to safety had been his only concern.

"Little Jul, what happened here?" Lita demanded.

"Oh, no," Freckles whispered, stopping by Julian and looking around in shock.

Julian couldn't blame her. "Vandals," he told Lita as he assessed the damage. The sofa had been sliced open and lay half in, half out the shattered window. Chairs had been overturned. Two walls had huge holes in them. Pictures had been taken from the walls and smashed.

"Vandals? You call your brother. He will come here. He will see...oh, how could they, those people," she said, and bustled over to the desk, muttering under her breath as she started picking up the papers.

Julian saw Manuel quietly walk in even as he, himself, started chuckling.

"What are you laughing at?" Susan asked, looking at him as if he'd lost his mind. And maybe he had. Still, Lita was putting it all into perspective.

"He laughs, *señorita*, because of my mama." Manuel grinned.

Freckles looked at Lita. Lita simply humphed and went back to rattling off in Spanish.

Then she looked at him. "What's she saying?" Freckles asked.

Julian couldn't help but relax. "She's praying that we all become best friends so this thing won't happen again."

"Friends?" Freckles asked in total disbelief.

"She's also quoting the verse about blessing those who curse you and that it'll be like heaping coals of fire on their heads."

Freckles finally understood and started laughing. Julian watched the worry and stress roll off her as her eyes twinkled and her mouth curved up into a carefree smile. Even her shoulders eased in relief.

"I think, Lita, that the prayer won't work if you're angry at them at the time. You're supposed to really mean it."

Again Lita humphed at Freckles. "I am praying in faith, *señorita*. I pray he will make us friends. He can change my heart just as he can that low-down snake's, too."

Freckles looked at Julian in surprise. "I don't know if I'm ready to pray that prayer yet."

Julian smiled. "Nor am I. However, why not let God handle this. He's the one who'll work it out. Not us."

Freckles nodded. "What now? Do we go into town to tell Mitch? Either way, it looks like the clinic won't be reopening today."

Julian shook his head. "No. I want to do this on my own. I don't need their help. Besides, Noble was drunk, simply blowing off steam. It won't happen again. However, if you want to go in and press charges for what he did to you…"

He trailed off and waited.

She shook her head, dropping her eyes. "I'd rather just forget it."

"Are you sure?" Julian asked quietly. "Just because I don't want the entire population of my brother's ranch out here guarding us doesn't mean you shouldn't report what happened."

Susan squared her shoulders. "It's in the past. Let's just leave it there."

Julian hesitated, worried. He wanted to help

her, and he wasn't sure her not reporting it was the best thing for her. Still, he wouldn't insist, simply because his brothers would overreact. "Okay."

"*Señor,* it will happen again. You know how he is. He does not like Mitch. Oh, he may not come again, but he will find a way to stop you."

Julian nodded grimly. "Let's just clean up. First things must come first. I want this clinic back open somehow today."

Manuel nodded and started picking up.

"This is so much like my family," Freckles whispered, drawing his attention.

"What's that?" Julian asked, wondering how this situation could remind her of family.

"Picking up. We all always worked together, each one of us having a job. The job got done that much faster."

Julian grinned. "Now, there is an idea. Why don't you organize us and get us all started on jobs that you think should be done so we can get this clinic cleaned up and reopened?"

He didn't like the way she stared at him. "Are you serious?"

"Yes, I am." He wasn't an ogre who didn't trust her—well, not exactly, he amended. "You said you came from a big family. So put those organizational skills to work.''

Freckles beamed with excitement. Despite his worry that she'd end up killing them all in the process, he fully decided that risk was worth it just to see her so excited. Maybe this would help her work out the fear and helplessness that Noble had caused. He could only hope.

''Okay, then. The most important thing is to get the lobby straightened up, the window covered and the medicine cart in the hall up and ready. Then we can make a clear path in the hall, and everything else, including the holes in the wall, can wait until after working hours.''

Impressed, Julian nodded. ''We're at your service, ma'am.''

''Okay, Hawk, will you handle the hall. Manuel, will you straighten the lobby. Lita, I'll help you with the receptionist area.''

Julian smiled and nodded before starting toward the hall. He couldn't help but overhear Lita as Susan approached. ''Don't worry, *chica,* God, He is in control. Everything will work out.''

Julian only prayed she was right.

# Chapter Twelve

"Why, hello there, Dr. Learner."

Susan turned and smiled at Mitch, who stood near her in the small clapboard church in Hill Creek, Texas. "You're not in uniform," she exclaimed, then blushed.

"We're in church, Freckles."

She made a face at Julian.

Mitch chuckled. "Well now, sometimes I'm in my uniform here. I dressed up today."

"There's a new widow in town. The new schoolteacher. Thirty. Petite…" Zach said walking up to the group with Laura and his daughter, Angela.

"Funny, big bro. Very funny."

"Just trying to make you feel at home," Zach drawled.

"Okay, Zach, leave Mitch alone," Laura chided, grinning up at her husband.

Angela giggled. "I'm going to go sit with friends. Hi, Dr. Learner."

Before Susan could reply Angela took off across the church to where a group of teenagers stood talking.

"Glad you could make it today, Susan," Mitch said, and moved past her into a pew.

Julian slipped a hand to Susan's back. "Shall we?" He motioned her in after Mitch.

"Thanks." She moved into the pew and took a seat. Watching the family together made her homesick for her own family. Their church back home would be well under way already. The two youngest would be in children's church and the two older ones would have been arguing over who got the outside seat before settling down to help with Rachel.

"What's the matter, Freckles?" Hawk asked her softly.

Glancing at him, she managed a smile. "I was thinking of my family and missing them. It seems like I've been gone so long and they're all growing up without me."

Julian tilted his head slightly. "You really miss them a lot, don't you?"

Susan nodded. "Yeah, I do. Watching your family only reminds me of how much I miss them."

Hawk nodded shortly, and she realized she'd pushed those buttons of his again.

"I know, Hawk. You can't wait to get out of here."

Hawk simply shrugged. "It's not that I don't love them, but I do want to make a name for myself."

Susan had started to reply when suddenly she stiffened in shock. "Noble is here," she hissed.

She knew Hawk had seen him by the scowl on his face. "Yeah. Well, at least they're here," he finally said.

Guiltily, Susan scolded herself for sounding so snobbish about them being in church when she, herself, wasn't perfect. "What's the old saying about the church being for sinners?" she said softly.

"How about He doesn't reject anyone, not one, but is here for all of us, Freckles," Hawk replied, and Susan could hear the reluctant acceptance in his voice.

"And if I didn't know better, I'd say you two

were overly angry at Noble this morning,'' Mitch drawled out quietly, for their ears only, having evidently picked up on their furious whispers. ''So, tell me, is there something I should know about?''

''Other than that Noble was drunk and came out to cause problems?'' Susan joked.

When Hawk stiffened beside her she realized she had done a no-no. Turning, she offered an apologetic look.

''What's going on? What happened?'' Mitch asked, suddenly alert and all sheriff.

Julian, tight-lipped, shook his head ''More of Noble's acting out against us. He was drunk and went a bit overboard. I've never seen him that bad.''

Mitch contemplated the two. Susan tried to appear innocent as she cocked her head and looked up at Mitch. Finally he grinned. ''It isn't going to work, Doctor. What I want to know is—''

The sound of the piano, guitar and drums interrupted him. ''Oh, look. Music. Time to sing,'' she said, and she started clapping in time to the music to discourage questions. Mitch gave her a knowing look.

They all stood, and Julian took the chance to

lean down. "Divine intervention again?" he asked softly.

Susan chuckled. "God does work in mysterious ways."

Shaking his head, he turned and started singing the song the music leader was leading them in. It had been so long since Susan had been in church. As they sang, she realized just how much she had missed the fellowship with other believers. The music flowed through her soul, reminding her of the love of God, renewing her, surrounding her in the presence of her heavenly Father. All too soon the music was over.

They sat down and the pastor started his message. Susan tried to ignore how old and tired she felt as she listened. When had she lost hope in the future? When had she started despairing that things would ever work out between her and Hawk or even her and her profession? When had she become so steeped in despair instead of in the simple joy of living and trusting God?

Listening to the pastor talk stirred something within Susan. He spoke of hope, of the future and the returning of Jesus and then about the trials and tribulations we face in our daily lives.

When he pointed out that God was in control and everything would work together for the good of those who served Him, Susan felt a bond within her break.

The fear of failure, pain of disillusionment and self-defeat all fell away, to be replaced by peace. God was in charge. She simply had to release control and serve Him and He would work all things out.

Then it was time for prayer. Susan couldn't remember a service she'd enjoyed more. As they prayed, she lifted her hands in thanks for the things God had shown her through the message. She felt years lighter.

Laura noticed it, too, as she walked up after the service. "I'm glad you came," she said, grinning.

"So am I," Susan replied.

Laura hugged her, and Susan returned it, realizing once again how much she'd missed Christian fellowship and acceptance.

"So you are coming over to lunch, aren't you?" Laura asked.

"Oh, well, I don't know...." Turning, she looked up at Hawk.

Hawk looked a bit uncomfortable.

"Actually, I have a lot of work at the clinic I really need to catch up on," she started, but Julian interrupted her.

"Yeah, we'll be there. The work can wait, Freckles."

Susan smiled, relieved. She didn't want to come between Hawk and his family in any way. But she'd thought it would be good for him to go and had even anticipated it herself.

"Great. I've always wanted a big family," Laura joked.

"Believe me, you might not," Susan replied, turning her attention to Laura. "I come from a big one and it's something else."

Julian watched the two women walk away, heads together as they laughed. Angela joined them and all three headed out of church. Zach, who had been talking to another group of people, turned.

And Julian was suddenly in between his two brothers.

"Okay, fess up, what happened at the clinic yesterday?"

"Something happened at the clinic?" Zach frowned. "I wondered what was up. Both you and Susan looked wiped out this morning when you walked into church."

Julian scowled at his brothers. "It wasn't that serious."

Both brothers simply stared. Man, how did they always do that to him? he thought.

"Okay, it was," he said.

Mitch's scowl turned dark.

"Don't start, Mitch. Noble and his goons came out and tore up the lobby. He was drunk, and I don't think he even knew what he was doing. The worst part, though, was he mauled Freckles."

Both men's features turned foreboding. "Was she hurt?" Zach asked, and though his voice and demeanor were mild, Julian recognized it for what it was—absolute fury. He'd seen that look a couple of times growing up, when he'd done some really stupid life-threatening stunts. It was a look Julian had hoped never to see again.

Julian shook his head, working to tread very carefully and not push his brother when he was this upset. "No, Zach. Just shaken. She doesn't want to press charges."

"Why not?" Zach demanded in a deceptively soft voice.

"Out of sight, out of mind, I think," Julian replied. "All he did was grab her and hint at things. I really think she just wants to forget and go on. Less public damage that way."

"Or," Mitch chimed in, "she might not want

to cause trouble in a community where she is the new person.''

''Possible.'' Julian hadn't thought of that. But in a town this size, she had to know everyone knew everyone else.

''Can I talk you into pressing charges?'' Mitch asked.

Julian shook his head. ''I really don't think that'd be a good idea, Mitch. All it'd do would be to cause more problems between our families. It'd look bad to the hospital, too. Besides, I can handle this myself.''

''By ignoring it?'' Zach asked.

''Yes. Noble was drunk and angry. It won't happen again.''

Zach started to say something, but Mitch shook his head. Julian didn't like it when they did that. Pushing past Zach, he said, ''Excuse me, but Freckles is waiting.''

''She does have a name, Hawk,'' Zach drawled.

Julian scowled over his shoulder. ''She is Freckles. She'll always be Freckles to me. So forget it.''

Zach laughed and Mitch joined in. Freckles looked up from where she stood near the entrance. He saw her look at him and study his face, then glance beyond him before looking back with understanding in her eyes. When he reached her side, she said sympathetically, "They ganged up on you about something, didn't they?"

"They always do."

"Teasing you?"

"Yes. And calling me Hawk."

"Ah," Susan said, nodding wisely. Turning to Laura, she whispered low, "I hope you turn Zach's life upside down for the next day or two for making my partner miserable."

Laura chuckled and winked at Julian. "You betcha. Let me go gather him up right now."

Julian's scowl left. "So that's how it works? Now, *this* could prove interesting."

"Uh-oh," Freckles murmured. "We've created a monster."

Laura laughed and walked off.

Julian slipped a hand to Freckles's back. "You ready to go? I want to stop by the hardware store and then head on out to the ranch."

"More supplies," Freckles said wearily.

Julian tried to reassure her. "It won't be that bad. We'll get it fixed up again."

He pulled the door open for her and helped

her into the car, listening as she murmured, "I know that now."

Going around, he climbed into the car and slipped his seat belt on. "What do you mean, now?"

The gentle smile she turned on him nearly took his breath away. "I mean, it's been so long since I was where I should be with my heavenly Father that today in church, He reminded me *He* will handle our battles. And everything will work together for the good."

Julian found himself relaxing at the soft glow emanating from Freckles. It put him at ease, shockingly enough. And it tugged at something deep and empty inside him. "Yeah. And God does promise when talking to Jehoshaphat that He'll go before us and fight our battles if we'll only praise Him."

"Exactly. I was so angry at Noble and really wanted to throttle him—"

"What!" Julian exclaimed, staring in shock at Freckles.

Freckles reddened. "I do get angry sometimes, Hawk. Anyway, I realized during church today my job was to forgive and forget. I'll talk to Mitch about the incident but not make a report. He can talk to Noble if he wants. Then I'll work on getting rid of my anger and let God change my attitude.''

Julian smiled. ''For me that's going to take a lot of work.'' He started the car and headed out of the church parking lot.

''Hey, with God, all things are possible. Even for stubborn-headed mule-minded people.''

Julian cast her a glance, having a feeling she was talking about more than Noble. But he couldn't see, for the life of him, what it would be. So he only nodded in response to her words.

''Well, then, I guess we just have to leave it up to Him, while we repair our clinic.''

''I guess so,'' Freckles said.

*We.*

What an odd concept. He and Freckles equaling ''we'' in any sentence. In any way *agreeable* or together in some way. The two of them agreeing to act a certain way. Unbelievable. Julian shook his head as he turned into the hardware store's parking lot.

Of course, Freckles had really surprised him over the past few days. Perhaps working together and being around her wasn't going to be so bad after all.

# Chapter Thirteen

"This is a wonderful roast, Laura."

"Angela cooked it."

Julian watched as Freckles smiled at Angela and said just the right thing to make his niece blush. "Well, squirt, there's something else you're good at," Julian teased.

"I'm good with horses, too. I'm going to be a vet," she informed Freckles for the third time in the past hour.

"Really?" Freckles asked with more patience than anyone else at the table had for the teenager, who had talked nonstop since sitting down. "I have a sister who wants to go into that field," Freckles added, taking another bite of roast beef.

"Oh, totally rad," the young girl exclaimed. "At first I wanted to be a horse trainer, but the more I thought about it, I decided a vet was a better job."

Susan chewed and nodded.

Her gaze hadn't left Angela's in the half hour they'd been at the table. She hadn't had a chance for it to leave the girl. That, or she was purposely avoiding his gaze for some reason. On impulse, he decided to draw her attention. Slipping his loafer off, he stretched his leg out under the table.

"And I am going to specialize in big animals even though I may not have the strength for some jobs, but I can get an assistant. I'm certain I'll be better with big animals. Will you go riding with me after the meal?"

Susan started to swallow so she could answer. Unfortunately, that was at the same minute that Julian ran his toes up her leg.

Had Julian realized what his impulsive action would cause, he wouldn't have done it. How was he to know she'd react that way? He'd thought a mild rebuke from her or maybe a kick. Still, they were talking about Freckles. Anything that could go wrong would go wrong when it concerned her.

In shock she stiffened and gasped—then choked. Her eyes widened and her hand went to her neck, but no sound emerged.

Alarm shot through the group.

"She's choking!" Laura cried out, and jumped up.

"Dr. Learner!" Angela said in sudden fear.

Mitch shoved his chair back and stood, starting around the table.

Zach himself, who was next to Laura, pulled Susan's chair back.

Susan gasped and wheezed, little to no noise coming out as she quickly turned blue.

Despite the fast reaction of those around him, Julian was around the table and the first to lift her from her chair. He slipped his arms around her waist and worked to remove the lodged piece of food from her throat. On the third upward thrust to her stomach it was dislodged, amid a clatter of relief and questions.

Julian turned Freckles in his arms, pulling her close. He didn't object when her trembling hands inched up around his neck, nor when her head sought and found a place to rest against his chest.

He was too unsteady himself to object. "You okay, little one?" he murmured questioningly.

The curly auburn hair bounced as she bobbed her head up and down. She whispered something, but he couldn't hear. "What?" he asked. leaning down.

"Th-th-that's twice now you've played d-d-doctor. You owe me a turn."

Julian burst out laughing.

"What is it?" Mitch asked. "Is she okay?"

"You ought to let her rest, Jul. Maybe that would help the shakes," Zach advised.

"I'm sorry, Miss Susan," Angela said, her face a mask of worry.

"It's not your fault, honey," Julian reassured her. Then to those around him he said, "I'm going to take Freckles into the den and let her lie down until she's over the shock. Doctor's orders, Freckles. Don't argue," he said when she started to lift her head to do just that. He wanted her away from everyone so he could really make sure she was okay, could ask her privately. Stingy, maybe. Possessive definitely. But he needed to do it. Bending, he slipped an arm under her legs and lifted her up close to him.

"Thank you," Susan said for Julian's ears only, her head still buried against his neck. "I'm so mortified."

"Anytime," he replied, and started across the

room. "And there's no reason to be, Freckles," he returned softly.

"Hey, little bro," Mitch called out.

Julian paused and looked back.

"You forgot your shoe." Mitch was looking pointedly at Julian's feet, emphasizing the fact that he wore only one shoe. Lifting his gaze he gave his brother a very knowing, big-brother look.

Julian felt himself flush. Refusing to reply, he turned and headed out of the room.

"Big brothers sure can be the pits, can't they?" Freckles said against his neck as he carried her into the study.

"Yeah," he replied, "they can. They love to make my life miserable."

"I'm sorry, Hawk," she whispered. "I just wasn't expecting it and reacted rather...badly. Why not try to take the advice you gave me about being mortified?"

Julian set her down on the couch. "I take it back. Be as mortified as you want," he said, and twisted his face up in a scowl. "As for reacting badly, I wasn't expecting to do what I did. I don't know what got into me. I simply acted on impulse to get your attention." Disgusted with himself and the fact his entire family knew what he had done, he said, "It won't happen again."

Freckles actually looked disappointed at his words. "But" *mumble, mumble* "Hawk."

"Why do you keep calling me that? And I missed part of what you said," he said as he shifted and sat down on the sofa next to her. He shouldn't really snap at her about his nickname. Others had called him that. It just sounded so different coming from her.

Her gaze turned tender and all soft again.

Warning signals went up. *Turn, don't look at her when she's looking at you like this.* But he couldn't do it. Suddenly his gaze seemed glued to the soft green eyes staring so lovingly up at him. "Because you are my Hawk. Many times, had it not been for your sharp eye, I would have had larger disasters than I did. To me, Hawk stands for something special, a protector, a strength...."

She trailed off. He couldn't blame her there. His hand had somehow ended up cupping her cheek.

"Hawk?" she asked.

"This attraction between us. Something I think we've denied until now..."

"I haven't," she confessed.

Julian glowered. "Well, I have." Her cheek was soft and silky. It felt fragile and so delicate against his large hand. "I think we should continue to ignore it."

"Of course, Hawk," she agreed.

"You concur?" he asked, surprised, his gaze traveling over the arch of her eyebrow, the angle of her cheek, the sweet, tender way her mouth curved when she smiled at him and nodded.

"Good. Then we won't worry. We'll just continue with work and not fuss about this. If something develops later..."

"But you said we should ignore it," she whispered, her own hand reaching up and caressing the back of his hand that cupped her cheek.

"Yes, I did. But if something happens, then we'll just deal with it later. I mean, our job comes first. Our plans for the future. Right?"

Susan nodded, stroking his hand again. "Right."

"Good," he uttered low, his hand shifting against her cheek. For some reason, he couldn't seem to stop touching her. Had Susan always been this beautiful, this gentle, this kind? When had she stopped being a klutz and become a person to him? Maybe as they'd worked side by side at the clinic to get it operational? Or when

Noble had touched her that day, scaring Julian to near insanity? Or was it only a moment ago when she'd started turning blue and he was certain he'd lost her? That had scared him more than he'd thought possible.

"What are you doing, Hawk?" she asked breathlessly.

His thumb stroked her lower lip once, twice and finally a third time before he lifted his gaze to meet hers. "Getting us both into a whole lot of trouble," he murmured just before leaning down and covering her lips with his own.

Her lips were undecided and ever so hesitant as she battled and then gave in to the kiss. She tasted wonderful, Julian realized. The simple kiss gave him a feeling of joy, peace, and home-coming. Hands inched back up around his neck. His own hands slipped around her waist and pulled her forward as he tilted his head and gave in to the need to deepen the kiss.

"Ahem."

Julian silently groaned. He broke the kiss and lifted his lips from Freckles, staring down at her. Susan's lips were wet and slightly parted as she gazed up dazedly at him. Finally he cut his gaze to Zach, who had interrupted them. "No damage from the incident," Julian said. Zach caught the double meaning and simply lifted a disbelieving eyebrow.

He saw the minute Freckles realized they'd been caught and something was amiss. Her eyes widened to saucers and she looked from him to Zach, who stood at the door, then back to Julian with this look of horror dawning in her eyes. "No. No, none. I'm fine. Perfectly fine. No harm at all. Just the clinic. Right, Hawk?"

Julian slowly nodded. Susan sure did chatter when she was nervous. Frowning, he realized she'd chattered a lot at him when they'd first met.

Zach smiled at her. "Good. I'm glad everything is okay. Angela was certain she said something to upset you and I assured her that wasn't the case. You'd simply choked but were okay now. Still, she insisted I check."

Freckles grew red. "I'm fine. I just realized something I hadn't realized, and well, in my shock I gasped and it was really silly."

Julian wondered if his older brother understood anything Freckles had just said. He sure hadn't. Evidently Zach did, because he answered, "Not at all. By the way, Laura is wrapping up the leftovers. She is insisting on sending them home with you."

"Thank you," she replied softly.

"Yes, tell Laura thanks," Julian added. "Now, if you'll excuse us," he said pointedly.

Zach grinned, but took the hint and left.

"Did he see? Please tell me he didn't see." Her gaze pleaded for something she knew wasn't true. She looked so adorable right now that he couldn't help but tease her.

"He didn't see," Julian parroted.

"Yes, he did!" she cried. Her hands gripped his arms as her face turned a deeper shade of red.

Julian chuckled and tried to soothe her. "Yes, he did. But you asked me to tell you he didn't."

Freckles smacked him on the arm. "You're awful."

"Ouch!" Julian laughed. "Yeah, I'm awful."

Freckles groaned and dropped her chin to her chest in utter misery. "I'm sorry."

"There's nothing to be sorry for." Julian reached out and squeezed her hand. "I'm just as flabbergasted as you."

"I'm not flabbergasted," she muttered. "More like astonished, shocked, bowled over, confused, disgusted, upset—"

"Upset?" he asked, unable to believe she'd said that. "Disgusted!"

"Okay, I don't know what I am. Your comments, though, aren't helping to stabilize my emotions. In my opinion, we should just forget it all and go on with our jobs."

"Okay. Sure." Julian wasn't sure why her words bothered him. After all, he was the one who always ended up crippled and walking around in agony whenever they were together. Still, her words irritated him.

Susan swung her legs around and stood, trying to hide her hurt and frustration. "Great," she said, unable to believe after all this time of caring for him that she'd just told him to forget it.

"Fine," he replied.

"Okay, let's get the dinner and go. We have a lot of work to do." But his words had upset her. Flabbergasted indeed. She'd flabbergast him. She'd figure out something to do to really flabbergast the thickheaded fool.

# *Chapter Fourteen*

"**B**aca-a-a-aw." *Thump.*

Julian groaned.

"Wake up, sleepyhead," Susan called through the bedroom door at the ungodly hour of 6:00 a.m.

"Did you open my outside window again and let that chicken in?"

The sound of pecking and scratching as the chicken made its way across the room to his bed told of its direct progress.

"Now, why would I do that?"

He could hear the amusement in her voice. "One wrong word, and the woman is going to make me pay for the rest of my life. How many days in a row does this make now that the chicken has ended up in my room?'' He thought about counting, but gave up, ''Why did I say flabbergasted? Why?'' he muttered, and went to shove the covers back—too late. Hester had made it up on the bed and landed on his abdomen—and stared.

Julian fell back and groaned.

Freckles's laughter floated to him, then her words. ''Come on, Julian. We have a patient, and I'm not waiting on you.''

*Patient?* ''Move, Hester. I have to get up.''

The chicken protested and he scowled, moving it aside before sliding from bed. Quickly he performed his morning rituals and dressed before leaving his room. Hester was right on his heels all the way. He tried to ignore her. The kids loved her. She had learned to flap her wings for treats when they said *Beg, Hester,* and she had learned to cluck for them on command—for a *special* treat. Julian shook his head.

The funniest thing of all was that the chicken seemed to like all the attention. And she hadn't laid a single egg.

Coming around the corner, he found Susan in the lobby with Manuel and a very pregnant woman. ''Manuel's wife?'' he asked Freckles.

"She's not feeling well, Doctor," Manuel said. He clucked around his wife before urging her back over to a chair. Manuel then went after the errant child who had come with them when they'd come in this morning.

"Susan?"

Julian was wanting to know why she needed his help. She was also a doctor, and he didn't think Manuel was the type to refuse her help.

"I can't make her understand what I want. I told her I need to do an internal examination and some other tests, but I don't know how to translate it for her and Manuel to understand."

"She uses words I don't know, *señor,*" Manuel said before going back over to his wife.

Julian watched, amused, and Manuel started petting his wife, fussing over her and helping her straighten her dress before pushing a strand of hair behind her ear. He had never seen a man quite so helpful before. "What words, Freckles?"

"Ultrasound, stress test, internal exam for effacement and dilation."

Julian turned and started explaining, gesturing, pointing to her, toward the back, to Manuel. Finally he turned back to Susan. "I think she understands."

But when Julian tried to get the woman to follow him to a room, a problem arose.

"What's the matter?" Susan asked, watching the young woman shake her head and grip her husband's hand.

Julian glanced at her. "She doesn't want me in the room." He grinned at Susan's astonished look. "I think she's embarrassed and doesn't want a man examining her."

"But surely with other children—"

"Mary Angelica, she had a midwife, *señorita.*"

"Oh." Susan certainly looked nonplussed. "Well, there should be no problem, then. I'll just take her in and examine her, okay, Julian?"

"You are a doctor, Susan."

The look on her face told him he'd taken her by surprise when he used her name. Grinning and deciding he liked teasing her a lot, he winked. "Enjoy. Manuel, you want to go in with her? Susan doesn't speak Spanish."

Manuel shifted uneasily. "I have never been in with an examination. Mary Angelica, I think she would like that." He turned to his wife and spoke to her.

Susan knew it'd be okay when the woman nodded, relief written plainly on her features.

Smiling at Julian, she said, "We'll be back in a bit."

Susan smiled at the dark-haired woman and motioned for her to follow. The young child wanted to stay with Hawk.

At the room, Manuel waited outside while his wife changed into a gown. "How many children do you have, Manuel?"

"Three, Dr. Learner. This will be our fourth."

"Any problems with Mary Angelica having the children?"

Susan started scribbling on the pad of paper.

"Oh, *sí, señorita*. She was in pain all night and the next day with the first one. With our second, she had him fast. But the third, she bled a lot and went a long time past when she should have had her."

Susan made notes. "Blood pressure problems? Anything like that?"

Manuel simply shook his head. "I don't know, *señorita*."

Susan smiled. "It's okay. Those are common questions." She pushed open the door and went in.

"Oh, *señorita*. They did make my wife get a shot after every child was born. Even when we lost one baby, she still had to have the shot."

Susan looked around sharply. "Rh factor?" she asked.

He shrugged. "I'm not sure."

Susan made a note to find out just where the baby was delivered and get the records. If his wife were Rh negative, she would be prone to more problems.

Manuel's wife sat on the table, the white gown around her and a sheet draped over her. The new nurse the hospital had sent over two days before stood near the head of the table. "Now, let's examine you," she said to Mary Angelica while Manuel translated.

Through the examination she found Mary was nearly forty centimeters already, which was normal for an eight-month pregnancy, and was swelling slightly. The worst part, though, was her blood pressure was high. Too high.

Susan made notes on the chart, mentioned to the nurse to try to trace down her chart. The nurse was then dismissed for the day, since they had decided to close early. Finally, she had Mary Angelica get dressed. Walking out of the room, Susan turned to Manuel. "Has your wife been having headaches, seeing lights before her eyes, dizzy spells?"

"Headaches, *sí*," he replied. "Why?"

"Her blood pressure is a bit high. You have to make sure she gets more rest. She's not due for six more weeks, and she's retaining some water. The urine test the nurse ran shows protein. Not too high yet, but enough."

"She isn't going to lose this baby, is she, *señorita?*"

Julian had walked up and now listened. Glancing at Julian, she hesitated then looked back at Manuel. "She shouldn't, if she takes care of herself. But it's very important she take time to rest every day. If she doesn't, she and the baby both could develop serious problems."

Manuel's brow creased with worry. "I'll see to it, Doctor."

Susan smiled. "Good. Now we'd better get breakfast before we start our work around here. After all, it is Thanksgiving, and we all want to get out of here before noon." She patted his hand and headed to her office. "Oh, Manuel, why don't your wife and child join us before they go home?"

"Thank you, *señorita,*" he called out, and hurried back down toward the examination room.

Susan went into her office and sat down. Julian followed. Looking up, she said, "I asked the nurse to track down Mary Angelica's chart."

Julian pushed the door closed. "So, what's up?" he asked, his brow furrowed with worry.

Susan shoved the chart across her desk.

Julian came forward and picked it up. Strolling around her desk, he leaned against it and began to read, his features turning darker the more he read.

"She's having problems. Would they listen if I told them to go to the community hospital and get admitted?"

Julian shook his head. "Manuel's very poor. He won't take any type of help. If you told him that, I imagine he'd refuse to bring her back in and probably quit here to stay home with her full-time until after the child was born."

Susan sighed and rubbed her temples. "Can we add her to the list we're making up of home visitations? I'd like to see where she lives and if there's anything else we can do to help her."

"Good idea."

"I thought we were poor where we lived," Susan said. "But this..." She pointed at the chart. "From what little I gathered the only food they have is what they can grow themselves.

And something about the roof leaking and where they sleep when it rains.''

Julian nodded. ''They're good people. But yeah, they're very poor.''

''Your family is expecting us for Thanksgiving dinner in seven hours.''

''Yeah. You sure you don't mind helping me fix up the last of the lobby before we leave?''

''I'm part of this clinic, too,'' she reminded him.

Julian nodded. ''Did you notice how protective Manuel was over his wife?''

Susan smiled. ''He loves her. Of course he is.''

''I suppose. I've never seen Manuel like that before.'' Julian shook his head. ''You know, Zach treats Laura that way, too.''

''I've noticed,'' Susan murmured dryly as she finished making some notes, closed the chart and stood. ''Love must bring out the protective instinct in men.''

''Did your dad treat your mom that way?'' Julian asked as they started down the hall.

Susan shrugged. ''I don't know. I never knew my dad. My stepdad did.''

''Oh, I didn't realize...'' Julian began.

"One more thing we have in common. Except both of your parents were killed."

Julian nodded. "And Zach decided to be both mother and father."

Susan paused outside the kitchen and glanced at Julian. "Let me ask you something, Hawk. Did it ever occur to you what might have happened if he hadn't become your mother and father?"

Julian seemed taken aback by Susan's question. Susan was sorry if she'd shocked him. But she could see it from the oldest sibling's point of view.

"What do you mean?" he asked, clueless as to what she was getting at.

"I mean, he had a life before your parents were killed. He could have let the county take you and Mitch away, but he took on the responsibility because he loved you. Maybe he's just been doing it so long that he doesn't know how to turn it off and needs some help learning."

"I know he loves me," Julian protested.

Susan smiled. "I know you do. Think of that, though, the next time you see him and Laura together, and relax a bit about his wanting you around him. It's all he's known for years now.

It'll take time for Laura to get him out of the habit—if she can.''

"It still doesn't change the fact I'm going to make it on my own with this clinic and then as a doctor out somewhere else."

Susan sighed. "Maybe not. But give him a chance."

Just as they started into the kitchen, the front door of the clinic slammed open. "We're not open today," Julian murmured.

"No," Susan agreed, and then in unison they turned and rushed down the hall.

Julian blanched at what he saw. Two men, holding another one between them, covered in blood, stood in the doorway. "He's been shot," the taller one said. "Right out on the range."

"In here," Julian ordered, and turned toward the first room.

The men were right behind him. Susan rushed on ahead and started pulling out instruments, calling for help from those in the kitchen.

But when Julian got him on the table, he knew there was nothing they could do for the man. "We don't have chest tubes or...it's too close to the heart," he muttered to Susan.

Susan pulled out a chest tray and set up an IV, running it into his arm. "BP is low," Julian said after taking it. "Still there, though." Seeing Manuel, he said, "Go call the hospital. We need him taken out as soon as possible." He was going to try his best, though, to save the man.

*"Sí,"* Manuel said, and ran off. Lita, bless her heart, moved right in and started cutting the clothes off the wounded man.

"What happened?" Susan snapped out at the two men standing there gaping.

"We were out riding, checking fences, in our truck. Bullet came through the window and hit him."

"Isn't this one of your brother's men?" Susan asked.

Julian nodded curtly. "Go call Zach," he told the two standing there.

At that moment the heart of the injured man stopped beating. Julian dropped the medicine he'd been about to push into the IV and started CPR.

He worked hard, Freckles right along with him, as they intubated and tried to resuscitate the man. But they just didn't have everything necessary for the procedure. No blood, no staff, since everyone was gone, their nurse having left only minutes before. Just the four of them plus the guests.

Thirty-five minutes later they called a stop. Both sweaty and exhausted, they pulled the sheet up over his head.

Susan looked up at Julian.

"Our first patient we've lost," he murmured.

Susan felt sick herself. Going around the table, she did the only thing she could think of, and that was what she did when her brother or one of her sisters was hurting. She hugged him.

Julian didn't hesitate, but wrapped his arms around her, taking support from her as he shuddered. "I'm so sorry, Julian. So very sorry."

She was affected, but hadn't been the one to make the call. Julian had done that. "You didn't make any mistakes. We just couldn't save him," she added.

Julian squeezed her tight and then pushed back. Reaching down, he cupped her cheek. "And how are you?"

She smiled softly at him. "Better than you, I think."

Her smile faded at the look of pain in his eyes. "Let's go tell the men," she said. She walked over to the sink to wash up and was surprised when Julian stopped her and turned her, giving her a light kiss.

"Thank you." He turned and started washing his hands.

"For what?" Susan asked, shocked down to her toes at his impulsiveness.

"For being there. I've lost patients before and have never, will never get used to it. But this...this feels like the first one all over again."

"I don't guess it gets any easier. We can only believe he is in God's hands now."

"Yeah," Julian said. "Ready?"

"Do you know...did he have any family?"

Julian paused. "A brother somewhere. I only know that much."

Not another word was spoken as they left the room and went into the lobby.

Julian wasn't really surprised to find his brothers there. Zach would take this personally. He cared about his employees. Julian didn't know all of them, but Zach knew details on every single person who worked on his ranch. Mitch, of course, wanted a report. Zach took one look at Julian's face and turned, hands on hips, head back as he stared at the ceiling.

Nerves causing him to tremble from head to toe, Julian walked forward. "There was nothing we could do. We still don't have all the equipment and probably won't be fully stocked until

January. Maybe if we'd had more equipment, but the bullet hit the left lung and if I had a guess, I'd say a major artery.''

His stomach roiled as he worked to stay completely professional. Susan, though pale, looked more professional than he did. His admiration of her soared. She had held together admirably. He'd never noticed how really strong she was. As he thought about that, he realized she hadn't tripped or knocked anything over in the past two or three days, either. Mitch's voice pulled his attention back to the situation at hand.

"What type of bullet? Can you tell, Jul?" Mitch pulled out a tiny notebook.

"I'm not sure. I can tell you that it was large for a rifle. Ripped a good hole in him.''

"We'll send him over to the hospital for an autopsy and they'll be able to give you more information, Mitch,'' Susan said softly, and nodded to the others in the lobby, particularly Angela, who sat by her stepmother holding her hands and chewing her lower lip worriedly.

"Laura's brother was shot, Uncle Mitch,'' she whispered. "You never did catch who did that, did you?''

Mitch grimaced. "We will, honey. Don't you worry about it.''

Zach finally turned, eyes damp, jaw working. "Will you all be over for dinner later?"

Julian looked at Susan, into her eyes, then nodded. "Late. We'll have paperwork to fill out, the hospital to report to. You guys go on. I'm really sorry we didn't have better news."

Lita took that moment to make herself known. "I knew Robby. He was a good man and loved the Lord. He is in a better place now. You do not worry, Zachary McCade."

Zach smiled at the small round woman. "Yes, ma'am, Lita." He turned to Laura and Angela and quietly gathered them, then one by one the lobby cleared.

When everyone was gone but Susan and Julian, he turned to her. "You did well in there, Freckles."

He watched tension drain out of her. "Well, right now, all I want to do is go collapse in my office."

He chuckled, a bit shakily. "Me, too. I guess we have paperwork to do first. The coroner should be here soon for the body."

Susan nodded. "So let's finish it. Then we can go be with our family."

"Freckles..."

Susan paused and turned back. She was surprised when he pulled her into his arms. He could feel it in the way she stiffened momentarily. "What you said about family?"

"Yes?" she said, and her soft voice seemed to vibrate through him.

"Robby had a brother. It's Thanksgiving. And now Robby's brother is all alone, though he doesn't know it yet."

He felt her small arms creep around him and stroke his back. He craved that gentle touch, the warmth, the feeling of another human being. "No, he doesn't."

"I'd hate for my brothers to find out on Thanksgiving like that."

Her head bobbed as her hands continued to gently stroke his back, lulling him, easing the tension from him. "Me too, Hawk."

"Sometimes this job is the pits."

"Yes, Hawk, it is," she agreed.

"And it makes you miss your family."

"Yes, Hawk, it does," she whispered, and he heard the tears.

Relieved now that she had released her own emotions, he allowed his own tears to slip down his cheeks as he and his partner stood in the lobby of Hill Creek Clinic and mourned the loss of a life they had both worked so hard to save—together.

# Chapter Fifteen

What was happening to him?

Julian flopped over to his other side and looked at the clock. It was 3:20 a.m.

He sighed.

The chicken made a noise over in the corner—probably a snore. He had no idea if chickens snored. But after running it out of his room three separate times, he'd decided to let it stay. It didn't matter, since he couldn't sleep anyway.

Julian looked back at the clock—3:22 a.m. Flopping back over, he stared at the other wall. He couldn't get the shooting victim of earlier today nor Freckles out of his mind.

She wasn't used to this type of life, yet had

worked with him side by side on a murder and held up admirably. She missed her family. She hadn't once complained about the emptiness of the plains. She was naturally clumsy. But she was one good doctor.

*Go on, admit it, that's not all you're thinking,* he silently chided.

No, it wasn't. He was thinking of how much he'd enjoyed her the past few days, how he looked for her to be there and how integrated she had become in his life. Though it hadn't happened just over the past few days. Looking back, it was as if he and Freckles Learner had been destined to be intertwined with each other from their first meeting.

He had done everything he could to avoid the woman. She had ''commitment'' written all over her. She was one of those women who wanted to settle down and have kids, and it was embedded in every movement and every word, every look that she made. That wasn't in his future. Or it hadn't been. But something was happening with Susan. He couldn't explain it, nor could he concentrate on anything else. Once he'd stopped focusing on all the bad things Freckles had done, he suddenly realized there were many good things and pluses to her he'd never noticed—or had pushed to the back of his mind to avoid seeing.

Julian flipped back over—3:32 a.m.

He groaned. He was never going to sleep at this rate.

When the coroner had come they'd helped him get Robby on the stretcher and given the man all the paperwork. They'd also submitted their reports for the hospital. Then they'd gone over to a subdued Thanksgiving dinner, where talk had centered on the recent drug ring that had been busted and speculation that Robby had been involved or had known something about some of the people who had escaped.

They'd driven back to the clinic in silence, very few words passing between the two. Julian had been surprised at how comfortable the silence was. They'd both retired early to their beds, waving good-night to Lita, who had just returned from her son's house.

But sleep hadn't come. He couldn't stop thinking of Susan. So, here it was 3:35 a.m. and he was going to get up and get a glass of milk because he couldn't sleep.

He sat up in bed.

Hester made a quiet sound of disgruntlement. He ignored her, pulling on a pair of jeans and a

T-shirt. Opening his door, he started out and paused. He'd heard something.

He hoped it wasn't Susan. He really didn't want to see her right now, not with his emotions all in a mess. *Father, do something here. I really don't know what I'm feeling and just can't face her like I am. Maybe I should just turn around and go back to bed....*

That's when he realized what he'd heard were the stairs to the upstairs. No one should be up there. They were using that as storage.

Alarm shivered up his spine and warnings sounded inside him. Somehow he knew...he just knew, Freckles was in danger.

"Protect her," he whispered harshly, and rushed down the hall. In the distance he saw a shadow and the shadow turned. He was fumbling for the light switch when another shadow appeared. "Freckles!" he shouted.

He found and hit the light switch. Nothing happened.

Freckles screamed.

A loud crash resounded.

Julian's heart went to his throat, and his entire body reverberated with terror. The back door crashed open. Someone ran out.

Julian raced forward.

"*Señor!* I see someone, a man, he ran from here!" Lita cried running in.

"Lita, get a lamp. Lights are out. Susan. I think she's hurt."

He slowed and reached down, feeling around for Freckles as he neared the spot he thought he'd seen her go down. "Susan? Come on, sweetheart, where are you? Tell me you just tripped or knocked something over. Please, honey, tell me it was just you being clumsy."

He found a leg just as she groaned. "I only wish," she muttered, and he nearly cried in relief.

He worked his way up her body until he could pull her into his arms. Then he held her tightly, shaking so hard he himself couldn't stand. So, instead he knelt there and held her. "You scared me, Freckles. You shouldn't be out of bed. Don't you know that? What were you doing out of bed?"

"I was getting a glass of milk. I couldn't sleep," she muttered, then groaned.

"No. Don't talk. Just rest. Lita! The lamp. I'm sorry. I didn't mean to yell. That hurt you, didn't it? I felt you wince." He knew he sounded like a babbling idiot, but he couldn't help himself.

"Did you see who hit you?"

"How'd you know it was me, Julian?"

"I was...well...my heart. I was talking and...with God, you see and..."

"Here we go," Lita said, and the bobbing light made its way into the hall.

Julian looked back and went weak-kneed all over again. "You're hurt. Oh, no. Your head is bleeding," he said.

"That's not a very professional diagnosis," Freckles said to him, attempting a grin.

He looked her right in the eye and said very softly, "I'm not feeling very professional right now. Lita, can you call Mitch? Tell him what happened. I need to get Freckles into a room and see to this laceration."

"We never have problems like this. Not until those people, they decide Hill Creek is a good place to smuggle drugs in. Two people in one day hurt. And before that, Laura's brother and, oh, I do not know, *señor*..." Lita muttered on and on as her voice faded toward the office.

"Can you stand?" Julian asked.

Susan sighed. "Yes. At least, I think so. I heard you, felt something whiz toward me and ducked. I'm not sure what the person hit me with, but Julian, had I not moved, he probably would have killed me."

Julian felt sick all over again. His knees buckled.

Susan caught him. "Hey, are you okay?" she asked, sagging back against the wall.

Her voice was full of concern. He laughed. He couldn't help it. Relief. Overwhelming relief. "Divine intervention again, Freckles," he whispered, and then he leaned forward and kissed her before deciding they'd both be safer just sitting on the floor until he was a bit stronger.

"What do you mean?" she asked.

He twisted and pulled her into his arms. "I mean, I had gotten up for a glass of milk when every bone in my body shouted you were in danger. I think the Holy Spirit had His gaze on you tonight and your time wasn't here to leave this earth."

She shuddered.

He praised God.

Finally feeling stronger, he stood. "Stay here just a minute. I'm going to go flip on the backup generator if I can find it. Yell if *anything* out of the ordinary happens."

"You don't have to worry." He heard scraping and movement and then she said, "I found something long and narrow here. Anyone comes near me without announcing who they are and I'll kneecap them.''

Julian chuckled. "That's my girl.''

He stood and hurried toward the stairs and down to the basement. He was careful as he went, listening and praying, hoping that whoever was there had gone for good. In minutes he found the generator and had it running.

When he returned upstairs, he helped Susan up and into a treatment room. Lita followed right behind them. "*Señor,* I checked all the windows and doors. They're all locked, but the back window there, it was unlocked when I checked it. *Señor* Mitch, he is on his way now. He was home, so he should be here soon."

"Thank you, Lita."

Julian looked at Susan. "It's a two-inch laceration. We'll give you some aspirin, do an X ray and then stitch it up. Then I want Lita in the room with you the rest of the night. Better yet, you should go to Zach's...."

"No. This is my home. I'm staying."

"Now, Freckles," he began, about to insist she go to Zach's.

"Don't you dare pull that 'now, Freckles' with me. I'm your partner and I'm staying."

He opened his mouth to argue, but she was

right. She was his partner. Why did he care so much if she stayed or not?

In a flash, like a two-by-four hitting him upside the head, he realized why.

He loved her.

He, Julian Hawk McCade, loved Susan Freckles Learner, the very bane of his existence.

# *Chapter Sixteen*

Julian sat at his desk during his lunch break, opening mail. "So, do you plan to go home after your stint here? Work in a city clinic, Freckles?"

Julian studied her carefully as she scanned the charts before signing them off. "Hmmm?" she replied, glancing up at him. "Oh, I don't know. I rather like it here. Two years is a long time. But when it's up, I might see about staying around," she replied noncommittally, and picked up another chart.

Julian looked down at the bill, set it aside and reached for the next piece of mail. "Really?" He frowned. He had pictured Freckles as wanting to leave, certainly not staying.

"Remember, I come from a hectic town. I find this type of life refreshing. I had hoped one day to get my family out of the situation they live in."

"I'm not sure you ever told me," he said softly, watching as she frowned, flipped a page, then signed the chart. She reached over, picked up her apple and absently took a bite.

"Oh? Well, yes. I've been saving what I could to pay for college for my brother and sisters. My mom and her husband didn't make enough for college. He was around just long enough to give mom more kids before he died of a heart attack. Anyway, I've been paying off my loans and putting away what I could. I hope to have enough for Chaseon and Chrissy to at least get started in college. They'll be able to help out with the others who decide to go. But first, I'd like to find somewhere they can find jobs, a place to live that isn't unsafe."

Julian simply stared, amazed. "You're planning to put your brother and all your sisters through college?"

She glanced up, surprised. "Well, I'll help them get a start."

"What if they don't want to go?" he asked.

She shrugged. "They should go. But I sup-

pose, if they really don't want to go, well..."
She thought a minute. "I guess I'd have to heed
their wishes. It'll be up to them. I can only help
them start. I won't ever make enough to put
them through and really, I don't think I should
pay their bill completely. They all need to learn
how to work."

"I didn't have to work. As a matter of fact,
you know, I never really questioned where Zach
got the money to put me through college." The
more he listened to Susan, the more he saw just
how stingy and self-centered he'd been these
past few years. *Father, forgive me,* he whispered
again—a prayer fast becoming a litany within
him.

"It came from somewhere, I'm sure, unless
Zach is into robbing banks."

Julian chuckled. "Not Zach. Now Mitch,
maybe."

That stopped Freckles from reading the charts.
She looked up. "Sheriff Mitch McCade?"

He grinned at the astounded look on her face.
Cutting off a piece of his own apple, he dropped
it to the floor where Hester sat near him. "Yes.
He was a bit of a lawbreaker before the old sheriff got hold of him. Straightened him right out,
the way I hear it."

"Oh, dear. I'll have to ask him about that next time I see him."

She smiled and Julian nodded. "Do that. It's one of my ways to get revenge on him for every time he comes out here to check on us."

"He's only worried," Susan said before getting up and moving the completed files to another table.

"Wanna do my files?" he asked.

She gave him a warning look and sat down to finish her lunch. "Not in this lifetime."

Looking down, he began to open another letter.

"Hey, Laura is here!" Susan stood and moved around her desk. "Hi, there. What are you doing here?"

Laura walked in, grinning. "I just stopped by to see how you were doing and if you'd gotten a chance to ride the horses."

"Every day," Susan replied, grinning. "So, what really brings you here?"

"Well, I'd like to talk to you, if I could, Susan."

Susan cocked her head and looked at Julian. He'd been acting odd all during lunch and she'd gotten the feeling something was on his mind. "I'll be right back, Hawk?"

He glanced up. "Sure. Hi, Laura," he said absently, and went back to doing the paperwork.

Shrugging, she walked out with Laura. "Why aren't you in uniform? Not working today?"

"I asked for today off. Besides, Christmas is in two days. We'll be closed the next two days. I wanted you to run a test if you would."

Susan frowned, touching the stethoscope in her jacket pocket. "What's up, Laura? Have you been sick?"

Laura smiled. "Yeah. But only in the mornings."

Susan caught on immediately. "You think you might be…"

"Uh-huh. Could you run a quick test to be sure?"

Susan grinned. "Of course." Going over to the nurse's station, she found one of the specimen cups. "You know what to do with this. Bring it back here when you're done."

Laura giggled. "Be right back."

Susan looked at her watch. It was almost one o'clock. Things were slow today. They could put up a sign telling people where to get hold of them if they were needed. The rest of the staff wasn't needed. Turning to the nurse at the desk, she said, "Tell everyone to take the rest of the day off. We'll see everyone back on the twenty-sixth.''

"Thank you, Dr. Freckles," the nurse said, grinning.

Susan groaned. "I'm never going to live that down, am I?"

"I think Dr. Freckles and Dr. Hawk has stuck with the kids. I'll go inform the rest of the staff. You have a wonderful Christmas."

Susan nodded. "You, too, Maryanne. Give your kids a hug."

"I will."

The nurse left just as Laura returned. "So, let's go check this."

Going back to their tiny lab, she put action to words and ten minutes later was beaming at Laura. "Congratulations, Mama."

Laura cried out and hugged her. "I have to go tell Zach, immediately."

It was then Susan registered just how she was dressed. "How'd you get over here?"

"Jingle Bells," Laura replied.

Susan gaped. "Oh, no. No way. You are not riding that temperamental beast back to the ranch. Zach would shoot both me and Hawk if we allowed that. Besides, did you notice how chilly it is out today? It's supposed to get colder.

What would happen if you got thrown? No, out of the question.''

Laura made a face at her. ''You're as bad as Mitch and Julian both, not to mention my husband. Okay. So how am I supposed to get home?''

''I'll drive you. I wanted to talk to Angela anyway.''

Chuckling, Laura nodded. ''Okay. You've got yourself a deal.''

''Let me go tell Hawk. Meet you at my car.''

Laura went one way while Susan went the other. She entered their office just in time to find Julian slamming the receiver down on the phone. ''What is it?'' Susan asked.

He looked mad enough to punch a hole clean through cement. ''They're going to meet in two weeks to consider shutting us down.''

''What?'' Confused, Susan moved forward, forgetting what she had to do. ''Who? Shut what down? We're licensed.''

''No, the clinic. The hospital board is contemplating shutting us down after the shooting. I can't believe it. What do they expect? We're a clinic! We're out in the middle of nowhere. Of course we're going to lose patients occasionally. They do, too. No one likes it. But it's part of life. With that and all the break-ins, they've decided this is probably a liability they don't need right now. I can't believe it.''

Julian slammed his hand down on his desk. Alarmed, Susan reached for it. ''They won't close it down. It's needed. Just think of the rounds we've been making to outlying people. Think of the people we have served here. Think of all the good that has been done in the past six weeks alone.''

''It's a political thing. It looks bad to lose people this soon. All of the publicity from the break-ins didn't help. Someone has started a smear campaign, saying the hospital is playing favorites because my brother is the sheriff.''

''Well, that's not fair!''

''No, it's not. And I'm going to go talk to them right now.'' Pulling open a drawer, he found his keys. ''Come on, Freckles. Let's go talk to them.''

''Oh, dear,'' she suddenly said. ''I can't. Laura is pregnant, and I am taking her home.''

''She...what? Laura?'' Dumbfounded, he stared.

''Sorry to drop the news on you like that.'' Susan winced apologetically. ''I just...she was going to ride Jingle Bells and I told her no.''

"Good idea."

"Why don't you wait, and we'll prepare and talk to them later."

Julian shook his head. "If I wait, Bate and his cronies will get a foothold. I have to inform Mitch what is going on."

Susan hesitated, then nodded. "Okay. Just be careful."

Julian nodded and rushed out of the building.

Susan found her keys and slowly followed. Laura was waiting for her. "What was that all about? He said, 'Congratulations, I wish I could watch Zach pass out when you give him the news,' then he hopped in his car and was gone."

"Bate Masterson."

Julian came spinning back and headed inside. "You women go on. I forgot something."

Susan nodded. "Let's put your horse up and then we'll go."

"What about Masterson? I've heard all about him from Zach."

Susan walked with Laura to get the horse and then crossed to the barn. "It seems the hospital is contemplating closure of the clinic."

"Oh, no!" Laura paused. "They can't. This clinic is important to the people out here."

Susan sighed. "It's Hawk's dream. He only

wants to do this to prove to his brothers he can stand on his own two feet.''

Laura led Jingle Bells into a stall and started removing the gear. ''He said that to you?'' Laura asked.

''He said as much,'' Susan replied.

''But doesn't he realize that by buying the clinic and taking the initiative, he has already done that? Or by deciding to go to medical school and making it all the way through he has succeeded? Or that there are so many other instances?''

''I think all he can see is that he's the youngest and that they have always taken care of him.''

''Oh, Susan.'' Laura shook her head.

Both paused as they heard the car leave the clinic again. ''So he's going in to talk to his friend on the board?'' Laura asked.

''Probably. That and…'' Susan hesitated.

Laura picked up on it. ''And what?''

''It looks like someone has initiated a smear campaign against Mitch, making it sound like the only reason the clinic was opened was to garner favor with the current sheriff and that the only reason it is staying open, despite all the bad things happening, is because of the sheriff.''

"Mitch is going to hit the roof when he hears that," Laura muttered.

"And I thought he was the calm one of the bunch."

Laura chuckled. "Not by a long shot. I'd say Julian is. Then Zach and finally Mitch. If you want to include my daughter, she comes in last."

"I like Angela."

"Liking her and realizing she is a handful are two separate issues."

Susan watched as Laura finished brushing Jingle Bells and giving it feed. "You really like that horse, don't you?"

"You really like Julian, don't you?"

Susan gasped in shock.

Laura giggled. "That answers that question."

Susan's shoulders sagged. "Is it that obvious?"

"That you love Julian or that he loves you?"

Susan shook her head. "Oh, no. He doesn't love me. But yeah, I meant are my affections obvious?"

It was Laura who stared flabbergasted this time. "Oh, come on, Susan. Of course he loves you. Zach and I have even discussed the propriety of the two of you out here together when it's obvious you're in love."

Susan gaped. "But...but we're doctors. Of

course we're going to live out here. And let's face it, Laura. Even if we did have feelings for each other—which Julian doesn't—when would we have *time?* It has been nonstop getting this clinic up and running."

"I can't believe that thickheaded fool hasn't said anything to you."

Susan trembled. "You're really serious, aren't you?"

"Yes. I am. It's times like these I'd love to smack Julian upside the head. Come on, get me home before Julian remembers he forgot something else, and I have a chance to smack him."

Susan giggled. "Don't you even think about it."

They both turned and started out of the barn. Susan grabbed Laura's arm at the same time that she stiffened. "A rider," Susan said, watching a horse racing away from the back of the clinic. "Who is that?"

"Stay here," Laura warned, and to Susan's astonishment she pulled a small revolver out from under her right pant leg.

"You can't go in there. You're—"

"Fire!" Laura interrupted, and rushed toward the clinic. "There's a fire!"

Susan stared in horror as she realized the back of the building was going up in smoke. Someone had set their building on fire.

# Chapter Seventeen

"Thank goodness Manuel is going to be okay," Laura murmured as she assessed the damage.

"Someone hit him pretty hard. He said he saw them, though. Do you really think… I mean, will they be able to trace it back to Noble?"

"Oh, yeah. We've been watching that one for a while." Laura frowned. "The clinic is going to be closed for a while, though."

"More than a little while," Zach said, hanging up the phone. "I just called the insurance adjuster and they're saying nothing was ever finalized because of the hospital contract. So it looks like, even though Julian paid to have insurance, it was never insured."

Susan felt dizzy with shock. "But…but he put every penny he had into this clinic. You know the hospital isn't going to replace the equipment he paid for."

Zach sighed. "No, they won't. And with the way Bate has been riding them lately, this will probably assure the closure. An understaffed, underequipped clinic isn't worth keeping open."

"But they need us."

"Not if you don't have the equipment. Sorry, Susan. You and Julian can go to work at the hospital, but—"

"You just don't understand, do you, Zach?" Susan said, upset that they were going to lose the clinic and upset that Zach hadn't seen what his brother needed. "Julian needs this clinic. This clinic is a statement to him, a way of proving to himself he can make it without your help. Working at the hospital will only make him feel he has failed. This clinic can't go under!"

Zach stared in shock. "You love him," he murmured.

"When'd you figure that out, Einstein?" Laura quipped.

"Sooner than it took you to figure out you were pregnant," he retorted.

Laura gasped. "You've known?"

Zach's shock over Susan's words faded, and he smiled at his wife. "Yes, love."

"Um, excuse me. About this clinic?"

Zach and Laura looked back at Susan startled, as if they'd forgotten she was even there.

"I have some money. If Julian finds out he's not insured, it'll kill him. Is there any way we could get on the phone and order the equipment that he paid for? Today, before he gets back? And I'll pay for it."

Zach frowned. "Do you have a list of what he paid for?"

"In the records. Fortunately, our offices weren't the part that someone torched."

Zach followed her into the office, an arm around Laura. When Susan pulled out the receipts, her face fell. "Oh, forget it. I can't afford this much."

Zach looked at the prices. "I can. I'll lend you the money. You can order everything and then handle it that way."

"What are you going to tell him about the insurance?" Laura questioned.

"I'll tell him I already called and everything is handled."

Laura shook her head. "Honesty is usually better."

Susan sighed. "I can't let him lose the clinic." The words *God is in control* floated back to her. But she just couldn't release this. How could God fix this? When she thought that, it hit her square between the eyes. She had never been able to let go and allow God to be in control. Here she was once again trying to fix everything. Wrong, wrong, wrong. She couldn't do it.

"You're right. Forget it. I'd better go out front to wait for Hawk. He's going to be devastated when he sees the mess."

"I'm sorry, Susan."

Susan paused to hug Laura. "Thanks. Now, go home with your husband. After all, he came all this way when he found out you were riding the range on that horse of yours. The least you can do is go with him."

"You'll be over for dinner Christmas Eve?"

Susan smiled. "Yeah." She didn't notice that Zach still had the receipts in his hand as she left.

# *Chapter Eighteen*

Susan was sitting on the porch when Julian returned. She knew he couldn't miss the damage. The south side of the wall was missing on Room Three, the room with the most loss. It just also happened to be their X-ray and lab section.

Julian jumped out of the car and sprinted toward the clinic. "What happened?" he demanded.

Susan stopped him with a hand to his arm. "Wait, Hawk."

Hawk paused, turning his shocked gaze down on her. She knew when he realized just what had happened. It showed in his eyes.

"It was set on purpose."

Hawk's shoulders slumped. Wearily he turned and dropped down on the second stair. Bracing his arms on his bended knees, he stared at his clasped hands. Susan had never seen anyone look more dejected. Getting up, she moved over and sat down behind him and began to rub his shoulders. Her fingers were cold from the chilly weather and she sniffed. "I'm sorry, Hawk."

"Why, Susan? Tell me why. All I want to do is make a success of this place. Why are Bate and Noble working so hard against me?"

"They have no proof Bate was involved. However, Manuel saw someone, and Laura is pretty certain they can trace it back to Noble."

"Manuel saw someone? Great. Where is he? I want to talk to him. Maybe it's someone I know...."

Susan's hands stilled on Hawk's shoulders. "He was hit pretty hard and has a concussion. They took him to the hospital. I didn't give him a choice. Money or no money, he was too sick to go home."

Julian muttered something under his breath. "The hospital will help pay. They have programs set up. And Manuel is a definite case of need."

"Which brings me to another problem. What

of Mary Angelica? Do you realize, tomorrow is Christmas Eve and her husband is in the hospital? She's missed her last two appointments, and when I went out to visit her the other day, I got…um…lost.''

Julian turned slightly and tilted his head in question. "What are you getting at, Freckles?"

"I know things look bad here right now. But, Hawk, would you take me into town before the stores close and help me put together a surprise package for the kids and mother for Christmas Eve?"

"Yeah. Let me look at the damage and assess everything. Then we'll lock up. Is that okay?"

Pushing her hair back out of her face, she nodded.

Hawk stood and then reached down to give Susan a hand up. On the stairs as she was, she was eye level when she stood.

They both paused, staring at each other. Julian reached up and brushed her hair back, his warm hand stroking her chilled cheek. "We're going to make it through this, Susan. And when we do, I want to talk to you about something."

Susan trembled from the serious tone in his voice. Her gaze touched every part of his face trying to discern what he meant.

He gave nothing away. Instead he leaned forward and kissed her gently before stepping back and moving around her. Susan couldn't give up touching him that easily.

She grabbed at his arm. "Wait up," she said, and wilted, relieved, when he slipped his arm around her and rubbed her shoulder. She smiled, joy burgeoning in her heart.

"You're cold," Julian said, heading into the lobby. "Next time, wait for me inside. What would we do if half of the team here at Hill Creek Clinic got sick?"

"Then we still have a clinic?" she asked, excitement rising.

Julian sighed. "We are supposed to have a meeting on the twenty-sixth about it. They are talking about shutting it down or going down to twice a week, since we don't seem to be very busy."

"Don't seem to be... Did you inform them that the nurses they sent weren't near enough staff? That we're spending twelve- and fourteen-hour days just trying to keep up with our paperwork? That if Lita didn't live here and put in extra hours, we'd be suffocating in an ocean of paperwork?"

"Yeah. And that's why they agreed to have

the meeting. They said if that was the case, they would reconsider. Records are being pulled now. They were led to believe we weren't that busy.'' He frowned, releasing Susan as he walked into the charred room. "The other major problem is all the accidents. They're certain the insurance will go too high out here and bring too much bad publicity.''

"But if Manuel knows who is behind it—''

"He can give Mitch his statement and Mitch can get to the bottom of it and—''

"Just maybe the clinic will be okay after all!''

"Yeah,'' Hawk said slowly. "Maybe, if we can replace all of this equipment. If the insurance can get it here in time so we don't lose the confidence of the patients. If-if-if.''

"God's in control,'' Susan whispered. "Just trust Him to work it out. We'll find a way.''

Julian nodded. "I'll have to make some calls.'' He looked at his watch. "I'm not sure who will be open at this time, but can you call Zach and tell him I won't be over there this evening? I'll make the other calls. And with luck, we'll be ready to go out to Manuel's around five or six. Okay?''

Susan nodded. "Sounds great.'' Then she remembered. Insurance. "Um, Julian? There's something I need to talk to you about."

"Oh?" he asked, turning.

"Dr. Hawk. *Doctoro* Hawk! Mama, she need you."

Susan turned just in time to see Manuel's seven-year-old daughter run up to Julian and grab him around the legs before bursting into tears.

"Oh, dear," Susan whispered.

"Get the medical bags," Hawk said shortly. "And extra blankets from storage upstairs." Then he bent down and lifted Mary Catherine into his arms. He didn't look to see if Freckles obeyed his dictate. Somehow, he found he liked holding this young girl in his arms. Comforting her. So tiny and innocent and so scared at the moment. He only wanted to take her pain away. "It's okay. We're going to take you back to your mama now. Okay? Mary Catherine? Okay?"

He continued to soothe her until her tears eased. "Mama, she is in pain. She find out about Papa and she hurt. Please, you help her," she whispered, and then buried her face in his neck.

"Of course we will, honey. You did right coming to get us."

Freckles came back with the cases and their

coats. "Let's go," she said, her face a mask of determination. "I put in a call to the local unit, but they're out on an accident on Miller Highway. It might take a while for them to get here."

She handed him his coat and slipped her own over her shoulders. "You might want to know what I found up there with those blankets," she said, striding out by Julian's side.

Instead of the car, he turned toward the stables. "What'd you find?"

"Hawk?" He heard the uncertainty in her voice, the way she hesitated before her footsteps turned to follow.

"Manuel's family is one of those families you just can't reach by car very well. If we take our car, believe me, it'll take twice as long to get to her. So, what'd you find?"

"Drugs."

Julian turned to look at Susan, coming to a complete halt. "What?"

"We know now why someone was trying to run us out of the clinic. Evidently someone had hidden quite a stash of drugs upstairs. In one of the rooms behind the storage boxes. They must have been using this clinic as a hiding place. I thought someone told me Mitch got all of those people."

"No. Not all of them. But he did think the trafficking had stopped. I have to go call Mitch."

"I left a message for him when I called the paramedics."

"We picked the wrong time to open up," he muttered, and started back toward the barn.

He heard Freckles pick up her pace. "We're going to ride.... We're going out there.... You have to be kidding?"

"Afraid not." Julian smothered a grin at Susan's shock as he set Mary Catherine down, and she ran over to a horse tied up near the barn. Tiny little legs reached and found the stirrup, and then she was on top of the horse.

Freckles laughed. "Life out here is never going to be normal, is it?"

He opened up the door to a section of barn that she hadn't been in yet and motioned inside to a beat-up old gunmetal-gray truck. "I used to drive this out on the range when I was a kid. I never got rid of it. Of course, I never thought I'd have to drive it this soon. I wanted to do some work on it."

Freckles stared, then burst out laughing. "All this time I thought if we had to go somewhere out on the range, we'd have to take the horses."

Julian grinned a slow grin. "Well, we could. But this will be much warmer."

She shook her head, chuckling.

The little girl rode her horse into the barn and then hopped off. Pulling it over to a stall, she expertly put it in and locked it up. Running over, she clambered into the truck.

"Well, are you ready, Doctor?" Julian asked.

Susan nodded. "Let's go."

The ride was bumpy, jostling and one she wouldn't forget. They had only one seat belt in the car—on the passenger side that hadn't been removed when Julian was working so diligently to make his truck as disreputable as possible. So Mary Catherine was strapped into that one.

Susan rode in the middle. Next to Julian.

As they raced along, Susan felt safe. Sitting there with him, next to him like this, she found she wanted to be nowhere else. This was where she belonged, here with Hawk, working with these people, working with him.

And she realized she had a decision to make.

She missed her family, had always wanted and planned to go back to them. But here, now, was where she should be. Whether Hawk decided to stay or not, when her time was up, she wouldn't be leaving.

She knew, though, that Hawk would.

Pushing that thought from her mind, she vowed to leave it in God's hands and concentrate on the emergency at hand.

As they arrived at Manuel's house, Susan studied it. More of a shack than a house, it wasn't any bigger than the apartment she had grown up in. The grass was brown from the colder weather, but it was well kept. On the east side of the house was a huge garden that went far back. Behind the house were some trees. She could see a tire tied to one. Shutters hung neatly on the windows. The roof was a patchwork of multicolored tiles replacing those evidently worn off or blown off by the fierce Texas winds.

When the truck stopped, Susan hopped out and hurried toward the front porch, being very careful as she walked up the weathered wooden stairs. The little girl ran ahead of her, babbling in Spanish as she did.

Julian conversed in Spanish with the girl as he followed Susan.

Going inside, Susan squinted into the dark and quickly found Mary Angelica.

"She's in labor," Susan confirmed. One look at her told the entire story. Face twisted in a grimace as she squatted and held on to the bedpost told them she was more than in labor. The water on the floor could be from a spill, but was probably from the baby.

"Julian, help me get her up on the bed."

Julian turned on the charm, murmuring as he helped the mother turn and lie down on the bed. "She doesn't want me here," he informed Susan as he helped adjust Mary Angelica.

"You are *not* leaving," she replied. "You tell her *I* said so."

He did and then said, "She wants her husband here."

"Tell her she'll see her husband soon enough. She's completely dilated, but...oh no."

"Freckles? What? 'Oh no' is not a medical term, Freckles. Want to fill me in here?"

Susan heard the banked tension in his voice. "She's breach. How in the devil did the baby turn in the last three weeks like this?"

Mary Angelica moaned.

Susan turned to Mary Catherine. "Sweetheart, can you get your brother and sister and go into the kitchen? Wait..."

She dug into her bag and pulled out a bag of candy. "Here, take this in there and share it with them. Your mama needs to have the baby."

"*Sí*," Mary Catherine said. Her gaze was

much too old for a seven-year-old. She knew her mom was having problems. She gathered her younger brother and sister with her and took them into the kitchen.

Mary Angelica moaned again. Susan quickly draped her and then slipped her gloves on. "Hawk, I don't know if I need you down here or up there," she said.

"I'm here, wherever you need me, Freckles."

Susan checked the positioning of the child once again. "I'm not sure she can deliver the baby like this. If we were at the hospital, we'd do a C-section. No, an ob-gyn would do a C-section."

Julian managed a chuckle. "Yeah." He murmured softly to Mary Angelica, drawing her attention to him. He brushed her hair back and started working with her to breathe.

"On this next contraction, have her push, okay?"

"Ah," Julian suddenly said. "Seems our little girl got it wrong. The mother has been having pains for two days. Her water just broke after she got the news."

"I'm not surprised," Susan muttered, and slipped her hand down and reached for the forceps. "Bottom first, little one," she murmured. "Coming out with an attitude."

Julian repeated the words to the mother, who grimaced and then pushed as her contraction started.

Susan pulled.

Julian helped her through the contraction, holding her and working with her.

Susan felt sweat prickle on her forehead and start running down her temples. "Again," she said.

Mary Angelica pushed again and then screamed as the baby came forth.

Susan quickly unfolded the baby and removed the cord where it was wrapped around one of the arms. Grabbing up a bulb, she suctioned the baby. "She's not breathing, Hawk," Susan whispered.

Turning her over, Susan rubbed her back, thumped her little feet and cleared the passageway again and was rewarded with a weak mew of protest.

"It sounds like she is now," Hawk replied, grinning.

Laying the baby down, she clamped and cut the cord, then handed the baby to Hawk before going back to work on the mother. The entire time, Hawk checked out the baby, talked with the mother, who was crying, and kept the kids off their mother until Susan was finished.

At the first cry, the children had come running into the room. Quite a scene. The first child she'd delivered with a slew of chattering kids running around her, no doubt. Susan straightened the mother's nightdress and covered her with a sheet. Then Susan went to wash up.

The aftermath hit her at the kitchen sink, and she trembled. She heard the door swing open and closed but couldn't turn around. She was afraid if she did, she'd disgrace herself with tears.

Warm, strong hands cupped her shoulders and pulled her back against him. "Congratulations, Godmama, we made a baby."

Susan laughed. How did Julian always manage to do that? Was this the same man who at one time used to run the other way whenever she was around? "I only delivered her, I'm afraid."

Julian's arms went around her, surrounding her with his warmth. "One of God's greatest gifts. I've assisted others delivering babies. Assisted on two C-sections in surgery, but that was it, until today."

Susan groaned. "I had never delivered one outside of a hospital setting. And none I delivered had complications."

"You did beautifully." His lips brushed her cheek and he paused. "Tears, Freckles."

She shrugged. "I'm just…happy."

"Don't apologize, little one," he whispered against her cheek. "Your spontaneous emotion is what makes you so special. I don't believe I said that," he added almost instantly on the end of his compliment.

Susan giggled. "I don't, either. You hated it and me when we first met."

"Hated? Oh, no, Freckles. I don't think I ever hated you." Turning her, he took her hands and lifted them to his lips for a brief kiss. Very softly, he said, "As a matter of fact, I think I knew somewhere deep down inside, all along, that I loved you."

"Oh, Hawk," she whispered, and in her enthusiasm, threw herself into his arms to kiss him.

That's how Hawk ended up with a broken arm.

# *Chapter Nineteen*

"So how did this happen?"

Julian groaned. "Hello, Mitch. What brings you out here this late?"

Mitch smiled over at the doctor who was applying the cast to Julian's arm and then at Susan, who was assisting him. "Got a call telling me my little brother came in with a broken arm. I was on my way home and thought I'd stop to investigate."

Julian stared at the plain white walls in the treatment room, his left arm resting in his lap, his right arm being held at a right angle above him while the other doctor worked to smooth the plaster strips into place. "As you can see, Mitch, I'm fine."

"Well, now," Mitch said, and pushed his hat back before strolling casually over to where Julian sat. "I don't know if I'd say you were fine. To me, a broken arm isn't fine."

"He's fine." Julian heard the panic in Freckles's voice and scowled at Mitch.

Mitch ignored him, studied Freckles a minute, then grinned. "So, it's finally happened."

Julian's scowl turned fierce as he immediately caught Mitch's drift. Mitch knew him too well. He was certain it was in his eyes how he felt about Freckles. However, Freckles must have surmised differently, for she blurted out, "I didn't mean to. It was an accident. There was a toy car on the floor. We had to bring Mary Angelica in anyway. Did you hear? She had a beautiful little girl."

"Lay off, big brother, or it's you that's going to be lying here."

Mitch chuckled. "I just got done visiting her. The baby is beautiful. Manuel is very proud."

Freckles shifted. Julian watched the way she kept a close eye on the doctor working on him and tried to listen to both him and Mitch. She was beautiful. He was in love. Everything was wonderful.

"I heard you were in here."

"Dr. Gonzales," Julian said, surprised. "What are you doing working this late?"

"You rest that arm," said the young doctor who'd worked on his arm. "Six weeks. Not a moment sooner. You can take it off then." Turning, the doctor left the room.

Dr. Gonzales waited until the other doctor was gone before closing the door to the room they were in. "We need to talk."

Mitch shifted, and Julian knew that look of instant alert. Susan must have sensed Mitch's sudden tension or heard the slight tone in Dr. Gonzales's voice, because she paused in washing her hands and moved over next to Julian.

He couldn't tell her how special her presence was next to him. Peace settled on him despite the doctor's tone. "What's up, Chuck?"

"It's about the clinic, son. I've been in a board meeting. And I hate to tell you this, but when information of the illegal drugs hidden out there leaked out, the decision was made to close the clinic."

Julian's entire world collapsed around him. Vaguely he heard Mitch say something, felt Susan's hand grip his shoulder. But he couldn't move. All of his plans...

"I do have some good news for you, though.

Dr. Weaver, who used to work here years ago, is over at one of the hospitals out near Denver. I just got off the phone with him and he has a position for you, if you want it.''

''But my contract?'' Julian's mind whirled. He'd just been told the clinic had been shut down, which should have meant he'd be stuck here for five years instead of two. And now he was getting the very dream he had wished for. He was getting to leave? He shook his head.

''Both of your contracts have been canceled. It was felt due to the danger you were placed in, because of the hospital's lack of planning regarding the clinic, that you should both have your contracts signed off in full.''

Julian thought, *In other words, the hospital is afraid that even though it's my property, they might somehow be liable. It couldn't have worked out better.*

''I'll get out of here, then,'' Julian said, thinking that he had finally gotten his wish. He would get out of Hill Creek. ''What would I be doing...oh, it doesn't matter. We'd be out of here.'' Julian turned and pulled Freckles into an embrace. His smile faded, though, as he realized the doctor had said nothing about Freckles having a job.

"What about Dr. Learner?" Julian asked now.

"We're still working on a job for her. Within the week hopefully we can have a place for you to interview with."

Susan smiled politely, more subdued than he had seen her. "Thank you. But I have somewhere else I can work if my contract is up here."

"Oh, Julian," Dr. Gonzales said, breaking off what was going to be Julian's query as to where she could work.

"Yes?" He turned his attention back to the doctor.

"You might want to tell Zach to put a hold on all the equipment he was ordering."

"What equipment?" Confused, Julian tilted his head.

"Oh, oh dear. I hope it wasn't a secret." Julian followed Dr. Gonzales's gaze to Freckles. She didn't look confused. As a matter of fact, she looked downright pale.

"What secret?" Julian asked.

"I'm sorry, dear." The doctor apologized to Susan and then turned to him. "Zach only told me he got the receipts for the equipment you installed yourself from Dr. Learner. He came in and reordered it today. Anyway, since you won't be needing it, he should know to cancel it.''

Mitch said something low and soft under his breath. Julian didn't hear him. He had turned, his gaze on Freckles. Betrayal raced through his entire body. ''You know how...''

''Well, now, excuse me. Get back with me tomorrow about that job. No, two days from now. I'll call my friend back then.'' Dr. Gonzales left.

''It's not like that, Hawk. He was mistaken.''

Her plea sounded guilty to his own ears. ''Did you give my brother the receipts? Did you offer to let him interfere in something that you *knew* I wanted to do, I *had* to do on my own?''

Her features twisted with guilt. Julian swore.

Susan gasped.

''That's enough, Jul. You don't go using language like that.''

''Stow it, Mitch.'' Julian slipped off the table. Turning, he looked at Freckles again and then turned and left.

''Hawk,'' Freckles cried out.

Mitch stopped her. ''Let him go throw his temper tantrum, Susan. He'll be home later. Then you can talk.''

Susan started to cry.

"Oh, now, don't do that." Mitch had never been comfortable with tears. Awkwardly, he pulled her into his arms. "Hush now, Susan. I'm sure he didn't mean to hurt you."

"I did give the receipts to Zach. But, but I changed my mind and decided to trust God that everything would work out okay."

His whole front was getting wet from her tears. But inside…inside he was getting indignant with what his brother had just done to this sweet little woman. Okay, she had broken his brother's arm. He'd heard the story. But at the moment, Mitch wasn't feeling any pity for him. Not with this poor little thing crying all over him.

"What am I going to do?" she whispered forlornly against his shoulder as the tears slowed.

Mitch stilled as an idea came to him. "Well, I might just have a plan, if you're willing to work with me on it."

He felt Susan stiffen and then she pulled back to look up at him. "A plan? You mean, you think, well, that I might actually be able to patch things up with Hawk?"

Mitch shook his head. "You don't have anything to patch up, honey. It's that stubborn-headed mule brother of mine that's gonna do the patchin'. He told you he loves you, didn't he?''

Susan's twenty shades of red was answer enough. "I thought so. It was written all over him," Mitch said.

"But I ruined it by interfering."

"No, honey, you didn't. He's upset. He can't see past the fact that Zach raised him and he is somehow dependent on him. He doesn't want us interfering. And now he's found you and is in love with you. What do you suppose he would do if you suddenly left for the job you said you have?"

"Oh, no, Mitch. I couldn't do that. I—I mean yes, eventually."

Mitch shook his head and grinned. "Immediately. Before Julian has a chance to stew. Zach has been too patient with that boy for years. I've seen Julian change and grow over the last two months since you've been here. He's grown from a kid into a man. But he still needs to learn that family is important. And I think losing you just might be what would finally get his attention."

"But, but, Mitch, I can't..."

"You want to help him?" Mitch asked bluntly.

Susan nodded.

Mitch smiled. "Honey, if it doesn't go the way I think it will, I'll make sure to tell him I ran you out of town for breaking his arm. Believe me, this will wake him up. It's time to get tough."

Susan hesitated, but that verse once again floated to her. God was in control. Trust in Him. "I wonder if perhaps God isn't using this situation to teach me to trust Him."

"And to teach Julian that family is important," Mitch added gently. "God always does have a reason for the things He allows to happen. Come on. I can get you out of here tonight if we leave right now."

"Now?" Susan squeaked in shock.

Mitch grinned. "Better effect on him."

Susan hesitated, then finally prayed, *Father, this is in Your hands. I don't know why, but I feel in my heart that Mitch is following Your lead here, so I'm going and trusting. Help me step out and just do it.*

Peace flooded her. Susan immediately knew she'd made the right decision, even if it was one of the hardest she'd ever made. "Okay, Mitch. Let's go."

# *Chapter Twenty*

Julian stood in the clinic looking around. "A job near Denver," he whispered. "Why doesn't that sound like a dream come true?"

Pausing at Lita's desk, he stroked the plastic top and then turned to look at the tiny little advertising plaques Susan had gotten to hang in each room. "When did this clinic become my dream more than my escape?"

"Maybe when you started doing some good."

Julian whirled. "Who's there?"

"Oh, I'm sorry, Doctor. I didn't mean to startle you. I'm Robby's brother. I went looking at the ranch for you and Zach said you might be out this way."

"Ah. Yes. I want you to know how sorry I am we were unable to save him." What to say to him when he had tried his hardest and lost the patient anyway?

"Thank you. It means a lot. I'm glad you had this clinic out here, and that you were the one who worked on my brother, someone he knew."

Julian shook his head. "Robby knew Zach much better."

"But, Doctor, it was you who was working on him, not your brother."

Julian felt as if he'd been hit with a two-by-four. "I, well, yes, it was."

"And I wanted to say thank you. If there's anything you need in the way of donations for this clinic, let me know and we'll see about getting something done. I have a thriving business. Robby didn't want to be part of it. I really could have used him as a foreman." He shook his head. "He wanted out, away."

Julian's heart beat loudly in his ears. The verse about entertaining angels unaware came to his mind, because this was just too familiar.

"They're closing the clinic," Julian heard himself say.

"What? Why?"

"Political reason."

"Well, I'll be...we'll see about that. The ranchers out in this area have needed a clinic for a long time. Son, I'm only two ranches over. This cuts my time in half if something happens."

Julian suddenly realized who this man was. "Liam Harford. I...well, yeah." Dumbfounded, he stared, shocked to his toes. He didn't know Liam was still alive. He'd only vaguely known Robby, but hadn't connected him with Liam.

"Robby was going by our mom's maiden name," he said as if reading Julian's mind.

"Ah. Well..."

"Don't you worry none, son. We'll see about keeping this clinic open."

"Thank you. Thank you very much."

"After all, if it weren't for the donations I made, half that hospital wouldn't be standing today." Liam chuckled and then came forward and shook Julian's hand. "Again, thank you for being there with my brother, even if you weren't able to save him."

Julian gazed up at the salt-and-pepper-haired man and nodded. "Thank you. Let me know if there is anything we can do."

Liam shook his head. "You gave me something to do, son. I have a mission now. To keep the clinic open.''

Liam turned and strode quietly out of the room, as quietly as he'd come.

Julian dropped down on the nearby sofa.

"I have been a total fool," Julian whispered. Remembering Robby and his death, he thought about how Liam had never had a chance to see his brother again, and then he thought about what the man had said. "I've been independent all along. I was trying to make myself an orphan, though. Oh, Father, I have been such a fool and so blinded.''

Julian thought back and realized that all of these years he had blamed himself for living and having a family when his own parents had died. Zach and Mitch had been his family. He broke down and cried. He cried for the loss, for all the years he'd caused Zach and Mitch grief. He cried until he felt the cleansing presence of the Holy Spirit fill him. Then peace came, a peace he hadn't known since before his parents' death.

It was dawn before he rose and headed for the ranch to find Susan. He wanted to talk to her, and hoped maybe they could work things out. He also wanted to see if she might consider staying on.

His mind was blooming with ideas until he walked into the ranch house and found both of his brothers and Laura all there. When they gave that look of impending doom, he knew something had happened. Something with Susan.

"Where is she?" he demanded.

Mitch shook his head. "She's gone."

Shock shot right through Julian, and he felt as if he'd just lost part of himself. "What?" he whispered.

Zach nodded. "You heard. She's gone." Zach paused, then walked over to Hawk and said with a small smile quirking his lips, "And I'm wanting to know what you're going to do to get her back."

# *Chapter Twenty-One*

*New Year's Eve*

Susan hurried home from the city clinic. She wanted to make it home before midnight. The streets were crowded. People were drinking and celebrating. After all, New Year's Eve was a time to rejoice with loved ones.

No, that was a lie. She wanted to be with Julian.

*Hawk.*

How she missed him. His laugh, his smile, even the wary look when she got overexuberant and ended up doing something that injured them both. The way he tilted his head when he was curious, how he rolled his eyes when Angela was telling one of her stories. How he always ended up getting up in the middle of the night to get a glass of warm milk.

"Your will, Father. Not mine. I'm trusting You."

That had become her litany for a week now. She was bound and determined not to try to fix this herself. Every time she did, it got her into trouble. Some things you just had to leave in God's hands. This was one of them.

Turning, she hurried up the stairs to her fourth-story apartment where her mother and siblings lived.

"Mom, I'm home," Susan called, going into the house.

She nearly tripped over the rug, though, when she saw who was sitting next to her mother, obviously chuckling over something her mother had said.

Susan blinked.

The entire room grew quiet. That raised chills on her arms. Her brother and sisters were *never* quiet. She blinked again.

No, she wasn't dead. The rapture hadn't happened and she'd been left behind. Julian was actually sitting on the sofa in her mother's apartment. Still, she had to ask, "Julian? Is that you?"

Julian stood. Susan ached to run and throw

herself into his arms. But that's how she'd broken his arm last time. So she simply stood there staring.

Julian finally broke the silence. "Don't tell me you've forgotten me already, Freckles, keeper of my heart."

"Oh, Hawk," Susan whispered, and, unable to help herself, rushed forward and threw herself into his arms anyway, deciding that's what two arms were for.

They closed around her. "This is where you belong, Freckles. In my arms. With me. Can you forgive me for being such a fool?"

Susan couldn't stop squeezing him. He felt so good, so warm, so relaxed. "What happened? You feel—different."

He chuckled. "Leave it to you, sweetheart, to feel the difference in me. I had never forgiven myself for my parents dying and me living. I did that the night you left. Forgave myself. I made up with Zach. My whole outlook on life has changed."

"Oh, Hawk, I'm so happy for you."

Pulling back slightly, she looked at him before running a hand gently over his cheek.

"I came here to ask you if you'd marry me."

Susan gasped. "I...oh, Hawk." Joy leapt in her before quickly being deflated. "I can't."

Julian smiled at her. "Why?"

Warily Susan studied him. This wasn't like the Julian she knew. "I can't because I have my family. Mom needs my help."

Julian turned, slipped an arm around Susan and led her across the apartment to the tiny balcony. "You can't help her from Hill Creek?"

"I no longer have a job there. Besides, Julian, I can't leave her. She needs help with Rachel. I'm sure you noted she has cerebral palsy. And...wait a minute? Hill Creek? But you got a job offer in Den—"

"I didn't take it. Believe it or not, things have happened in the week while you were gone. Bate is no longer wielding such influence. A long story there. His son has been arrested and is awaiting a trial. And the clinic is ready to re-open. We have a new friend on the board who is determined to see the clinic is done right. He's even donated all the equipment and then some to make this a first-rate clinic."

"You're kidding."

"All they're waiting for are the doctors to open it."

Susan felt sick to her stomach. "I can't leave them."

"I know, love, just as I realized I couldn't leave my own family. I'm supposed to be in Hill

Creek. I don't know why, but that's where my destiny lies. As does yours. Zach is giving me a piece of land that has the old ranch house on it. It needs work. But he and Mitch offered to help me fix it up. It's big enough for us, and all your siblings and your mother.''

''Oh, Hawk, you can't mean that,'' Susan protested, unable to believe what she was hearing.

''We've already discussed it. Your mother has agreed to come live there. She said she'd like to work at the clinic. And I'm sure one or two of the kids might be able to help there, too. If not, there are ranches hiring summer help in a few months and there are always jobs in town. But best of all, they'll be with you, and out of here— one of your dreams, if I recall?''

Susan cried. She couldn't help it. Tears flowed freely as she threw her arms around Julian and hugged him.

''So, what do you say?'' he whispered against her ear, holding her close.

''I say...''

A bell in the distance sounded.

''Yes,'' she whispered, and kissed him.

''Happy New Year,'' he said gently, and cupped her cheek. ''What a way to bring in the New Year.''

''Happy is right. And whether it be a new

year, or not, Julian, I love you. And I vow to you now I will never stop loving you, but love you forever."

"And I you, my love. From this moment on with God as our guide."

Then Julian pulled Dr. Freckles Learner into his arms and sealed their New Year's resolution with a sweet, gentle, all-consuming kiss that was filled with promises of the joy to come.

\* \* \* \* \*

*If you enjoyed Cheryl Wolverton's*
*FOR LOVE OF HAWK, you won't want to*
*miss the latest from Steeple Hill's*
*Love Inspired...*

*The heartwarming and very lively series*
**FAIRWEATHER**
*from three exciting authors:*

*WHAT THE DOCTOR ORDERED,*
*by Cheryl Wolverton*
*On sale February 2000*

*TWIN WISHES, by Kathryn Alexander*
*On sale March 2000*

*BEN'S BUNDLE OF JOY,*
*by Lenora Worth*
*On sale April 2000*

Dear Reader,

"Trust in the Lord with all your heart and lean not unto your own understanding." It sounds so simple but is so very hard. As humans, we want to fix everything ourselves and steer our own destiny. We think we know it all, not realizing sometimes that we see through a glass darkly and there are reasons behind things that happen. How many of us have experienced what I'm talking about?

I know when I was very ill a few years ago, I couldn't understand at the time, but I realize now that God was teaching me to trust Him and not to depend on myself, that my existence came from Him. In this story we have two doctors, Susan "Freckles" Learner and Julian "Hawk" McCade. Both must learn to let go of the past and simply trust God. Of course, lessons are sometimes hard to learn, and what happens if the only way to learn that lesson is to end up with the bane of your existence getting assigned to the same clinic where you work?

Hawk thinks someone is out to get him when Freckles shows up. All he wants is to get out of Hill Creek, Texas. He never expected to fall in love. Freckles has been head over heels in love with Hawk from the beginning. The only problem is, when she's around him, she becomes very clumsy. From all the bumps and bruises and near broken bones, Julian has become wary of Susan. Sometimes it just takes letting go and allowing God control for things to finally work out. And when God puts two people together, you can be sure He'll work it out.

I hope that you enjoy the book. I'd love to hear from you! Let me know what you think.

Cheryl Wolverton